THE

Misfits

THE

Jimmy Santiago Baca

Arte Público Press
Houston, Texas

The Misfits is published in part with support from the National Endowment for the Arts. We are grateful for its support.

Recovering the past, creating the future

Arte Público Press
University of Houston
4902 Gulf Fwy, Bldg 19, Rm 100
Houston, Texas 77204-2004

Cover design by Mora Des¡gn
Cover art by Gronk Nicandro

Cataloging-in-Publication (CIP) Data is available.

♾ The paper used in this publication meets the requirements of the American National Standard for Information Sciences—Permanence of Paper for Printed Library Materials, ANSI Z39.48-1984.

22 23 24   4 3 2 1

For all those who keep trying to get it right.

CONTENTS

WALK THE ICE

————

Dorothy was right, there is no place like home. But if you don't have a home, only an apartment or flat, there's dozens like them. I've moved into many while migrating from city to city for jobs. In that situation, the closest thing to home are the friends you make where you're at. As you move on, some friends get lost and others remain in touch.

For five years I lived in LA writing screenplays. I considered staying until I was overwhelmed by the feeling that I needed to change my life and move back to Santa Luz. I was hoping to reconnect with old friends. And that was how I found myself on I-40 east heading to Santa Luz.

No more reminiscing nostalgically about the cool morning, the homemade tortillas and simmering pinto beans and red chili, the *huevos rancheros*, the music and murals and friends—I was stepping back in time. Although I wasn't returning, down on my luck or broke, I made the decision to leave LA at the height of my successful writing career because I needed open space uncluttered by traffic and mobs.

I couldn't delay my departure and risk the chance of becoming one of those writers who stayed, who kept promising to leave, taken in by the sumptuous mountains of money that became too much to resist with time. It's easy with money, power, privilege to drowse into an eternal torpor, after which, years later, you find yourself regretting never having fulfilled the youthful promises of working for a studio and making enough money to carry you through the time necessary to write the book of your dreams—a novel about your estranged relationship with your father. By the time I had met too many who complained of never writing it, too many lulled by riches. They got complacent and comfortable, always thinking there was still time, even though they knew in their hearts they had sold out and betrayed themselves.

It's tough to be a writer, and almost impossible to get your life unwrapped and set out in a disciplined fashion to sit down and write every day. I needed a quiet, unexciting place, and it seemed Santa Luz was just country enough and slow-paced enough to give me a chance at my dream.

For most writers it just doesn't happen, unless rich relatives come to your rescue or loads of grants from the foundations and other benefactors pitch in to sustain you while you write. Otherwise, it's a long, arduous road most cannot endure. But I was determined.

I couldn't compromise my writing for grants and didn't have wealthy relatives. I felt an urgency and used my own cash to get back and set up my office in a nice, old, crumbling adobe house off Don Onate Street, where I'd throw a few pinon logs into the stove and start my long-awaited novel.

On the way, I stopped in Gallup to eat a plate of blue corn enchiladas. As I scooped up the chili and eggs from my plate, I knew I had made a good decision. And if the delicious food wasn't enough, I was sitting in one of my favorite small cafes, packed with Mexicans and Navajos gabbing and laughing. The menu hadn't changed and the café had maintained that certain fragrance of prairie life. I knew I belonged.

I drove on, open cacti and sage lands and long expanses of high desert prairie and mesas. Billboards advertised "real Injun artifacts." Snakes. Turquoise. Truck stops. Casinos. I turned the radio on and flipped through the stations: on NPR a special report of a famous #MeToo movement Latina writer living in Mexico turned out was a fraud—her accusation lies. It was all about a big payday. More stations—mass immigration swelling at the borders, Russia invades Ukraine, Covid, Trump moldering with prostitutes in a south Florida swamp, a bloated oligarch buys a soccer team for his son's birthday present and four NYC penthouses for his mistresses, Putin murders women and children and a crown prince in Saudi Arabia executes eighty-one dissidents in one day. Bolsonaro chars thousands of acres of Amazon jungle, killing off indigenous tribes to make room for cattlemen, oilmen, lumbermen and mineral predators. The Wart, North Korea's Kim Jong-un, wants in on this freak sideshow and is deploying missiles again—the miscreant will try anything to get attention.

I turned the radio off, promising myself to stop listening to news. I was pleased with the silence as it sank into my soul. I could hear the sweet sounds of the desert again, feel them, the raw, dry vibration of vegetation, crows, all of it coming back to me, heralding my return, even though home I sensed was not what it used to be.

It never is. The world had grown much smaller with all the constant deluge of information. I felt like throwing my iPhone out the window. It wouldn't do any good—I still had my laptop packed in the satchel.

It was snowing in Ukraine, I was going home, and in my own way, I felt a little like one of those refugees lumbering out of cratered cities, reminded then, as I write this now, how once I was a kid living in Santa Luz, my little heart bursting as potential petals were unfurling, leading me to a generous world.

So much chaos was happening in the world, and people desperately trying to hold it together, huddling in rooms stockpiled with weapons, peering out windows in disbelief, weird climate patterns ravaged the land—snow in Florida, hurricanes in Kansas, drought and fires in LA. . . . Time was no longer flowing but smashed and rushed up against us, pinning us like butterflies against walls of flames and floods and urban drug-overdosed corpses.

At some point during the Covid pandemic I became afraid of living life, hesitant to trust it. It was not what it seemed. Who knew in what shape and with what dangerous intent from every corner it would spring at me from the shadows? I even found myself questioning whether I should take the dogs for a walk.

It was like, some years ago in another time and place, that moccasin I saw curled up in a rock hole on top of a boulder I was standing on to watch the river flow by. I wanted to prove to myself that I was courageous, so I rolled out my blanket and decided to sleep right in the way where I knew that snake would come out at night to hunt for field mice. But after an hour or so, I rolled up my bedding and got the hell out of there, admitting, no matter how hard it was, that I wasn't that courageous. In fact, no matter how you looked at it, I was a coward.

In a sense, I kind of felt that same way going home.

On another occasion—when I first met my wife twenty-five years ago—I found myself in a similar situation. That time, I wanted to prove to my girl how much I loved her. I wanted to prove my belief in our love to her and show it was blessed by the Divine Forces of Nature that rule this Earth. There was so much magic in our relationship that I was willing to risk my life and walk out to the center of an icy pond. I just knew, even if it cracked, I would not fall in, because an angel would hold me up. That's the kind of faith I had in the power of the universe. Otherwise, how was I to explain me having the loveliest girlfriend in the world, how to understand her love for me, that seemed to go from where she sat, down into the Earth, exiting on the other side, wherever that was? . . .

I had never had this love, the invincible feeling I got with her there smiling at me, conveying the most profound truth of what happiness is as she looked at me. It does not happen: a girl twenty-

five years younger, from a Mormon background, hooking up with
an ex-convict Mexican Indian—it just doesn't happen.

My pride has always handicapped me. I've always lived outside any perimeter society has set up. No fence or wall has been
able to contain me. I've always, always found a way around or
under or through whatever obstacles are set before me to restrict
who I am. No better image than a trail of open and discarded
handcuffs exhibits my journey's wake. In prison I did it with writing. In society I did it with success as a man who is drug-free,
not a boozer, kind and generous, a homeowner, financially
blessed, happy, has healthy kids, is able to handle most situations
that come his way in a rational manner . . . In short, I'm pretty
damn proud of myself. And I must add, although I approach life
with humility, there was a time I couldn't bear to look at myself
in the mirror. With time and spiritual practice I learned to love
myself and realize how I'm a good-looking a man, I am caramel-
skinned, Mexican Indian, Chicano by choice—and self-love ra-
diates from my demeanor.

I expected when I got home, there would be a sense of ful-
fillment, of deep satisfaction that would reinforce my sense of a
hard-won victory and balance. I expected that coming home
would be a sort of final piece to the puzzle of my being staunchly
placed in life, but surprises were in store for me.

My wife and I were once sitting in Taos, New Mexico, having breakfast on the deck of an outdoor café, and a waitress came
up and asked us if we were movie stars—I kid you not—if we
were starring in the movie they were shooting there. We smiled
and said no, but we looked at each other with raised eyebrows; we
looked like movie stars. We smiled, kissed, went back to our
room and made love for a few hours. Wherever there was a place
available, we made love—creek beds, rivers, mountain tops,
caves, in the car—you name it, we did it there. We were traveling everywhere, enjoying life. Once when we were making love,
a red bear crossed in front of us, padding west. Eagles and red-

tailed hawks soared above us, white-tailed deer walked the soul-inspiring countryside and swelled our hearts with awe.

I've been in planes that almost collided in midair; others a yard from landing had to veer nose-up because the wheels didn't come down. I lost everything in two house fires. My car stalled with an oncoming car racing at me 95 miles per hour; I was sitting in the middle of the road sideways staring as it barreled down on me, so close I could see the driver's frightened eyes begging me to move. At the last minute, his eyes turned tragic and he swung sharply left to the embankment to avoid me, his car flipping and exploding. A strange kid pulled a knife on me at a crosswalk and a stranger next to me grabbed the knife and knocked the assailant down. I skidded off a mountain cliff in a rage. I gambled with gangsters in life-and-death misunderstandings. I was hunted by FBI agents with a shoot-on-sight order—they had my most wanted poster in post offices. I was ambushed by a dozen police and escaped in a shoot-out. I overdosed three times on heroin. I had a heart attack on cocaine twice.

And now, owing to my trust in God (none of the conventional Gods you know) who brought this woman into my life, I consider all these near-death misses a ritual passage to get here at her side, even though, when we went to meet her parents in South Carolina, they said upon meeting me, that a Mexican was never welcome in their house. While she visited her folks, I rented a room at the Motel 6 five miles away. When I picked her up, her mother yelled from the door, "Come around again and we'll shoot you." I smiled and waved, thinking they'd have to pay me an awful lot to counsel them out from the dark age into modern-day society.

And now, late December, just south of Santa Luz where a large body of water and ice had pooled at a massive hole, to test my faith in the powers that made this love mine, to show my gratitude for this woman who had given me my greatest happiness, I decided to walk out to the middle of the pond. I picked up a large rock and hurled it out to see how thin the ice was. It landed and cracked a spider web. Millions of white little bubbles emerged like cells just beneath the ice along the cracks. I picked a larger rock, two hands to lift and launch it. It hit and slid, and larger cracks crept out in every direction.

I turned and glanced at her and smiled. Behind her, in the distance, sat the dark planet known as the Martinez steel mill that we had visited earlier. How lucky am I to be a poet, not to be laboring over a molten pit of iron. I remember the galvanizing department; mostly Chicanos, Mexicans and Puerto Ricans amid the smoke and sulfuric acid fumes clouding the air so thick you see others walking only by the beams of their hard hats. A crane man way up was moving tons of molten vats, pouring them into a cauldron large enough to fit school buses. The men hand-dipped hot strips into batches of molten zinc. Men worked the hot tongs. Everyone drank whiskey with their lunches.

For them too I would walk the ice. In honor of my grandma and grandpa, fieldworkers, house maids, janitors, cooks. In that mill was an army of men and women who made cities and yet lived unnoticed. My warm breath blew into the cold air. I stared at the ice. I stood at the edge of the pond, the city of Santa Luz beyond me, home of our state capitol, home of the famous Chicano poet Antonio Baca, who I had long adored. In fact, I worshiped most of his poetry, which inspired me when suffering from writer's block.

I remembered the other day, Stace and I, with three steelworkers, drove to Baca's house. The streets were packed with two feet of snow. I found the run-down house on a street corner, with graying decrepit clapboard; it had been taken over by dealers and crack addicts milling around on the porch. It was a letdown, but understandable in a country that hates poets.

I drove by slowly, my steelworker friends in the back seat nervous as the crack dealers glared at us. I turned left at the corner and got stuck in the snow. My wheels spun, I gunned it, the tires whirred. I stuck the automatic gear shift into reverse, then drive, threw it back into reverse, then drive, rocked it back and forth; the transmission whined, tires smoked and spun hot on the snow, transmission and tires zinging like two giant yellow jackets around us. I slammed the gas pedal, accelerated hard, let up, revved the pedal again, shaking the car back and forth, the whole while studying Baca's tar-papered roof and splintered railing and ancient thick windows burnished blue by sunlight. I watched as three, then four and five crack addicts moved our way and surrounded the car.

One of the three men in the back said, "Go, move this goddamn car!"

"Let's go, get us outta here, let's get the fuck gone," another steelworker ordered.

Four of the druggies stalked within arm's length of the car, grinning at their prey. The car lurched and lifted up, the tires belching black snow up in the air and the engine steaming and grunting as we slid and careened down the street, fishtailing as we all laughed and said, "¡Ay ay ay!"

I had never been so in love with a woman as I was with Stace sitting at the picnic bench by a cheap barbecue grill with a metal overhang. There were no facilities, no water fountain or bathroom in that park. When in love, one needs nothing. Really, even as cold as it was. I could strip my coat and shirt off and be as happy as if fully clothed in an Alaskan parka and puffy insulated pants. That's love, and it makes the air vibrant and good to breathe and the gray day full of happy possibilities.

The men in the mill skim the heavy hot slag off the surface of the molten zinc melted to 850 degrees, wielding ninety-pound iron spoons to dredge the burning vat. That's the shit.

I looked up. The overcast day made the Martinez steel mill look that much darker and menacing in the distance. I knew the workers used this picnic area sometimes. Maybe this was as good as it got for them. Their vacation was this place, where they played with their little girls, snuggled with wives as their hotdogs smoked on the grill, where their teenage sons fell in love with their friends' daughters, where they came and drank away their sorrow with other trailer park friends. The barrenness of the place felt like their decaying lives. Only in a place like that—with tufts of dying grass and weed patches and gravel walkways and a swing set whose paint was peeling—could a man appreciate the laughter of an infant or the kiss of a young lover.

You can keep artsy-fartsy Paris. Give me the arthritic man with swollen knees, sipping his Jack on a bench, who thinks and worries and dreams about one day making a comeback, one day . . .

I was in love, out of control, like too much gravy over mash potatoes. You know, where you get to mash your fork full of gravy and mash potatoes into your peas and corn and stuff your mouth. That's love.

I was someone who didn't belong, a raggedy cluster of road-side field trees that didn't belong to anyone and grew all by themselves away from people. I was the kind of kid roaming around on a boring afternoon with a drinking poppa long gone and a momma in bed on her fifth boyfriend. I was like an ugly winter tree for people who had lives that didn't fit into anything, lives that felt more like an ex-wife throwing your clothes at you as she chases you out of the warm kitchen, lives that yelled your sorrow at you like a train a few yards beyond your window, passing in the night, rattling all about your decline and disappointment. I felt kinship with the trees whose trunks were twisted young in a tribute to forced loss of innocence, to a horrid legacy. I grew thick and onerous. Fifteen, maybe twenty tree trunks gnarled together is how I loved her. Holding the fence line, baby, I was holding the fence line against the winds of racism and poverty and failure that wanted to blow me down.

It was the kind of love that took James Dean around that curve too fast, made Bukowski wear his boxer shorts while drinking and writing poetry, the kind of love that makes a man go down

on his knees a coward. And in the inner-bark grow rings where I
had the whole universe encircling me, running like a vein of gold
beneath the glinting barbwire buried in my bark . . . That's how
I loved her.

It's how her love made me bigger and crazier and made me
lose myself in her vast array of roads, where parts of me took off
walking, each part waving goodbye to the others, a dozen mes
starting off a hundred ways in her—that's how love was. I could
start from any point in the compass and still find center, come at
it from anywhere—plains, mountains, deserts, seas, forests, Artic
and Sahara, tropical and moonscape—and I ended up where I
was supposed to be, in her arms. That's love.

I never get lost yet don't know where I'm going. No matter
where I'm at, I end up . . . if you're in love, it's the center.

I stood there at the Martinez Pond, at the iced edge of the
pond, feeling like I was at the center of the universe.

Earlier that day, touring the mill with my girl, we saw fire on
a level and scale equal to the fire God used to make people and
Earth. We saw the darkness of that fire, the vast worlds of dark
rafters, a six-story-high warehouse a mile long, piles of steel
shavings, ash, epic cauldrons where metal was liquefied—metal,
molten red—poured into giant molds and forms and shoved into
furnaces so formidable they tamed a landscape as open and broad
as New Mexico into a city like Santa Luz.

These epic men worked forces that fashioned the future, destroyed dreams; matter immune to all else but their will. It is
smudged a man's heart, became a worker's Lent ash thumbed on
the forehead at Mass with courage undefined and hurtful.

A steelworker, Gutiérrez, told me a story of a man pushing a
wheelbarrow across a plank bridge to dump the ash into a molten
pit of bubbling metal, and the wheelbarrow leaned too far to one
side and, in straightening it out, the weight was too much, and
instead of letting it go . . . he tightened his grip and followed its
momentum down into the molten steel. Something in him, a steel

part of his will, said, "No, I will not let this lead me to its will, I will not surrender to it," and he died in this very human heat of conviction.

And then there was Gary, walking his daughter across on her first day to register at New Mexico Highlands University. He didn't say much, but his eyes did. He was used to carrying his scuffed black lunch bucket and thermos and felt awkward. His eyes saw the steel beams that held the buildings up, saw the bicycles racked up, the new cars wealthy parents had bought their kids, everything that was made of steel, everything he had helped make.

He was close to retiring, hoped that he didn't get sick like most of the men and women, who retired only to cancer, joints rubbery with arthritis, headaches, bad blood—the effects of putting in decades at the mill. It was all worth it now as he escorted his daughter to her first class.

He drove a truck, lived in a trailer, was a steelworker all his life. There he was, walking beside her across the lush grounds of the university, shy and quiet, proud but wordless. He had worked all his life in the mill so that his daughter could walk those grounds, sit in one of those classrooms and read books his savings had bought her. His hand was on all of it, the way it was when she was a little girl and he fixed her room up with butterfly posters and flowered quilts and dolls and stuffed bears. This was her new room, a woman's room.

He'd never been late for work, never was the cause of an accident. That was worth more than a million dollars to him. The school grounds were too quiet. At the mill people talked into microphone speakers to each other. The quiet at the university was eerie. His world was midnight shifts, black coffee and enough prescription pills to make it to his pension. National Steel fucks the workers. But then what corporation doesn't? And Americans, stupid as they are for new trucks and guns and boats, ignore the abuse. Rectangular buildings a mile long, safety helmets, safety

glasses, safety boots—but no safety for the heart or the soul, as
it is slowly squeezed out of the body, no safety from coffins that
most suit up early, after having given their lives to the company.

My pops said once he could place his index finger and spin a
compass needle, and wherever it landed, to the smallest line in-
dicating a direction, he could look and tell me an experience he
had there. The same with the roulette table marble.

"You'd be blessed," he said, "to claim the same." He went on:
"Don't you ever sit and get complacent because you're comfortable. Test yourself, boy, push yourself, even if you fall over the
edge. Otherwise, you'll live but won't have a life. We call that
zombie living." He died in the gutter, a hole the size of a quarter
in his liver.

I looked around, spotted the largest rock and picked it up. I
heaved it like a shot put. It hit the ice and slid a good twenty yards
to the center of the pond. I turned and yelled to Stace, "I love
you."

Traumatized by taking risks all my life, even from altar boy
days when I drank the wine and ate the host like a saltine cracker,
so thirsty and hungry was I, I stepped on the ice, stopped. I
stepped a little ways, stopped. It was so cold, the ice had already
furred the surface where I had thrown the rocks. They had slid
across the ice like my own life sliding, sliding, sliding away from
society to the center where few dare to go. Most lives are lived
close to the banks, but few risk themselves to step out where nothing is guaranteed. Grooves, little channel cracks webbed out like
a fisherman's net. Another step. Beneath the ice, little bubbles
floated up, like something slow boiling down there in the dark.
Like there was a body down there, letting out small burps or farts.
Something rose from the depths, emerged with white claws and
fangs and waited beneath for me to fall in. The clear dark skin of
the ice monster below glistened and creaked as it followed me,
ready to emerge as I stepped. There was a heart down there beat-

ing, some deep foreboding warning me to turn around, turn around now.

I stepped forward, and this time my weight sent movement in the cracks, the ice shivering for a second, cracks zigzagging out in longer trails. More zigzags. The web grew. I felt like a fly in a spider's web, enticed but unaware of the spider coming for me. I looked up and saw the big rock, still a ways to go. I could make it. Beneath my shoes, a paperclip stuck to green water weeds that licked the bottom of the ice plate. Metallic razorblades of ice shimmered below.

I turned. Stace was watching. I took a step, and a crack sounded like a zipper being zipped. Thin layers of ice bits freed themselves and floated under my shoes. Ten minutes had turned into a year. I stepped again. The ice tightened like a cable dangling in mid-air. I could hear the give. It was about to snap.

The ice gripped against my weight. I could feel its clenched fist losing its hold. I leaned down and felt the ice with my fingers, and it burned like acid. Women and kids watched now from the pond's edge.

The ice coughed below. Breathed. Its rattles thickened. My legs were freezing. The cold raked through my jeans. My knees were stiff, my ankles brittle. It was the kind of cold that broods in the bones. I stepped to the rock, and the cracks followed me now like a blue uniformed policeman crouching on one knee, a pistol ordering me to stop. "Fuck you," I said, "chase me." The ice made the sound of a thick bolt being wrenched. It was creepy, and I knew it was the prelude to an ancient door opening. I was going in.

Water froze as soon as it escaped the cracks.

I could not back down. I cursed. I should have never fucking done it. It felt like the cold was pinching my toes. The air smelled like rust.

I turned and smiled at Stace. Her smile was so beautiful, I said, "Fuck it, game on."

Below the ice, black whorls spun purple ribbons of water that clung to the underbelly of the frozen glass. I stepped. It splintered. I stepped, shards broke off. My legs trembled. I stepped, cracks ached in every direction. I shook a little. A cold wind flayed my face. I stepped, the ice bristled.

Only five steps from the rock, there was a gurgling from below and water seeping up through the ice. Pops told me Christ was speared in the ribs and crowned with thorns, but nobody ever wrote about the tears on his cheeks. He had all the power to make those crosses bend down and release those two crucified beside him. But he didn't. He cried. I felt that crying in me then, but I held it back. I felt the power of his tears, and the power of forgiveness and prayer. I was numb with humility, with a repentant heart.

I picked up the rock and, as the ice split into chunky sections, I lunged back and crawled on my belly toward Stace, using the weight of the rock to propel me like a diver with his light. I had landed hard on my chest, elbows and knees. I slid to Stace as freezing water burned my hands and cheeks red, numbed my fingers stiff. Behind me, trays of ice tried to catch up to me, slapped against each other, knocked and clunked, then floated off.

I dropped the rock at Stace's feet and said, "This is how much I love you." It was my way of finding the words.

᪣᪣ ᪣᪣

Years later, I gave a poetry reading at a university and a professor from the English department gave me a ride back to my hotel. We passed a dark city to my left. It was something out of George Lucas' *Star Wars*, a bombed-out alien city on a planet that ceased to exist long ago. There was block after block of black warehouses, padlocked and protected by an endless, rusted cyclone fence with numerous No Trespassing signs.

"What is that?" I asked.

"A steel mill," she said, "closed. Used to be thousands of people worked there, a whole town of people. People got married in it, babies were born, families grew, generation after generation, then the boys on Wall Street sold it and . . ."

I remembered the Martinez steel mill and my walk on the ice.

Her voice hung in the air like a broken rosary, each bead bouncing down a marble staircase into a dark basement no one ever visited.

We drove and the buildings continued on. It was a city within a city.

"What happened to the people?" I asked.

"You wanna see them, they're right over there."

"Let's go."

She turned right, and we found ourselves driving around a neighborhood where men sat on porch steps drinking, teenagers wearing hoodies hung out on the streets, dealers waited on corners for approaching buyers . . . radios blasted, voices clamored, stray dogs barked as they scuffed through curb trash, unaccompanied little kids roamed the alleys.

All I could think of were the stories they had that would never be told. It was too depressing to let pass. People can't just work all their lives and then be thrown away and forgotten. They can't just disappear without telling their stories. They just can't not matter.

"All these people used to work there," she emphasized.

The scene reminded me of one of those war movies that depict cities bombed to rubble and people stumbling about dazed and blank-eyed. It made no sense to me; the idea that our business and government leaders would let this happen was unconscionable. In the truest sense, I felt whoever was responsible had gone mad, like the Joker in *Batman*, up in a high-rise somewhere, his red lips sliced into an eternal grin. I felt evil resonating off those black, corrugated steel warehouse walls, an evil responsi-

ble for a whole tribe of lost souls wandering the wasteland of
crime, addiction, sexual abuse and alcoholism.

We drove out, heading for my hotel, when I asked, "Where's
the office for the steelworkers?"

"What do you mean?"

"The main headquarters."

"I don't know."

"Can you find out?"

She looked at me, searching for a reason why I was asking,
pursing her lips, then answered, "I can try."

"Great. Let me know by morning. I'll cancel my flight for to-
morrow."

～∽ ∾～

That's how it started and how I ended up the next afternoon
in Merrillville, Indiana, the next afternoon, standing before a desk
to ask a secretary if I could speak with the head man for the steelworkers. And just as I was asking, a loud voice from my left
boomed, "Hey, I saw you last night on the Bill Moyer's special,
'The Language of Life,' reading poetry!"

I turned and saw three huge men walking out of an office.
They were brawny NFL linemen, tall, barrel-chested, thick, like
massive brick buildings. The one who came up to me had a full
gray beard, large hands, long legs—he was a Viking in a suit.

"Well," I said, as he approached and his body seemed to take
over the whole room, "can I talk to you?"

Strange how things happen. Because a long time ago I agreed
to let Moyers interview me for his PBS special, I now found myself in the national steelworkers' director's office asking if it
might be possible to facilitate a writing workshop for steelworkers to write their stories.

The giant-of-a-man said, yes. His name was Harmon. He was
a no-bullshit brilliant, compassionate man. He was certain that
all the steel mills in America would soon be sold out to foreign

interests, and he needed to do something to transition the men and women from the work they knew into new occupations. That meant getting them an education and helping them learn to write and express themselves.

A week later, he flew in about thirty steelworkers from all around the country. He put us all up in a motel for the next month. Every day, we met for three hours to talk about their experiences and figure out how to write about them. At a minimum, what they felt was important in their lives would not be lost and could be printed up and given to their kids as a gift describing their mothers' and fathers' journey in life. At best, the writing would be good enough to get a publisher to produce and distribute their work nationally and for the workers themselves to go on tour to read at bookstores.

The very first meeting we had with all the workers was held in a drab, industrial, cinderblock room with lockers lining the walls and harsh florescent tube lighting running the length of a corked ceiling. They sat on steel folding chairs while I fielded questions and explained the format of the classes. We set up a series of goals and discussed how we would achieve them. It would be lots of fun. I explained Stace would be helping me, since her father worked all his life in the steel mill. I didn't tell them that I hoped her family would accept me once they knew what I was doing with the steelworkers. (During the course of this workshop, her father actually received his monthly steelworker's newsletter announcing our project and exclaimed aloud, "He's all right." But to her mother, even after a decade, I was still "a piece of shit ain't got no business here ain't no American ain't nothing but a damn foreigner. . . .")

Everything in the Q&A went fine until a woman sitting toward the back raised her hand and stated, "There's always folks like you that come here saying you're going to help but all you do is steal from us, take and take. What's to prevent you from stealing our stories and making them yours and making money off them? That's what always happens, we get screwed."

My eyes skimmed the still, questioning faces of the workers, and I could see that most of them accepted the fact that I was doing this out of compassion for them and anger for the way they'd been treated. But it was evident that they, too, reserved a morsel of doubt and allowed that I might also be, if not someone exploiting them, then someone intent on deceiving them.

I understood. I myself had similar feelings about my publishers, who paid a pittance for my poetry but lived high on the hog.

I took a closer look at the woman, her white age-freckled arms . . . and I knew her. She had wiped a lot of snot from noses. Washed a lot of dishes. Bathed a lot of kids' backs and legs and crotches and ears and hair. But I didn't know the eyes, the cruel and hard grey/blue agates that looked on the world with nausea. She wore the cruelty of an ugly woman once beautiful. The ugliness of the world had made her lean and mean, made her cheeks sink and her face wrinkle, her voice gravelly and rough as the kickboards workers use to shake snow off their boots before entering a bar.

I saw all this in her white arms, her skinny neck pocked with blackheads, her puckered lips parched from too many dusty bus stop pickups and late arrivals of kids that always seemed to need her help. She had dusty gray/blond hair as ill-kempt as the sand after people have littered the beach with trash. One side was held in place with a child's simple barrette, her hair pasted to her small skull as if she'd used her spit to palm it down before entering the room.

On this woman's bony shoulders the entire liberation of women in the mill rested. Imagine me in a comfortable room with big stuffy chairs and a leather couch and a table with finger foods and wine and juices interviewing for PBS the most formidable feminists who fostered the women's movement. They're all beautiful—the Jane Fondas and Gloria Steinems, with lifts that make their eighty-year-old faces appear lopsided with fleshy lips and tight cheeks and sharp jaws, their eyes as aged as pigeonholes on a Manhattan rooftop. Imagine me asking them questions about their activism and involvement in getting women to free themselves from men's powerful enslavement, and the whole time I'm thinking I'm talking to the smartest women on Earth. But then, here was this steel-working woman who had labored to care for her kids so they'd have something to eat and a roof over their heads. I asked myself, who was doing the real business of saving our communities?

You can't eat words or pages or fancy catch phrases.

So, this woman stood up, wearing jeans and a T-shirt, and pulled out a copper union card from her back pocket and said, "They gave me this 'cause I'm the third generation to work at the mill. When I started, more 'n thirty years ago, I only wanted to pay off a new truck and then go to school and get a good job. But then I stayed on to pay for my kids' college . . . six kids, all paid by me." She paused to fetch her wallet and opened it to a picture taken when she started at the mill; she was beautiful. "That's what I looked like when I came in . . . and the mill took it all from me, every last goddamned drop of my looks, my youth . . . my hope. And I wouldn't trade it for nothin', 'cause it also paid for my kids to have a better life.

"So, I ain't in no mood to hear 'bout how much you care about our stories. My tears been gone a long time ago. There ain't none left. When it comes to your good-hearted bullshit, we got a saying here: 'Put some ketchup on them potatoes and serve 'em up somewhere else, to someone still driving the highway searching for their dream.' Here, they all been burned up in that furnace out there . . . along with our lives. I don't mean to rain on your sensitivity session here, but the amount of sweat we've given could drown a whole country of do-gooders."

I got to know Janice—that was her name—and she eventually trusted me enough to give me one story, one that I've carried with me all these years.

Steel mills are small cities and they create traditions—crew picnics, ride-along buddies—for decades, during which time friends share their woes, birthdays, baptisms, marriages, medical problems. Steelworkers and their families get to know each other because for many it's the best job they'll ever have and it creates a lifestyle dependent on the mill paycheck. As with all societies, traditions come in good and bad rituals. Janice said men had a hard time accepting women into the mills, and for a period there in the beginning, they did everything they could to disable any woman from even thinking of coming in, including rape.

Janice started on the graveyard shift, and the chief put her to shoveling the ash in the silo into wheelbarrows and dumping it in a slag pile. It was normal for her to endure all the flirting and sexual harassment the men inflicted on her daily; it was part of the job, and she never complained. She cursed them, belittled them, told them to fuck off. They wished they could fuck her, ". . . but they were so ugly that even their mommas would leap off bridges if they could sober up a day to see what monsters they had spawned."

One evening they sent Big Jack, a bulldozer of a white man down into the pit with her. The workers knew he was a savage who had raped many women at the mill. They figured that Janice needed a lesson because she acted like she was above them all with her defiant attitude.

"We'll just see about that when they come back up out the silo, we'll just see if she's still so uppity."

Sure as a turkey gobbles, as soon as they hit the bottom of the silo, Big Jack grabbed her around her throat, hurled her back and slapped her down. "Take your clothes off and turn around, bitch." He wanted it from behind, then up front, then her mouth—he was going to get it all.

Leaning on her shovel, she got up off the ground and knew that if she even tried to hit him with the shovel and landed a smack with all her might, he'd only blink—he was that huge and violent.

A single electrical line swung down between them with a bulb that swung like a pendulum, making their faces shadow, light, shadow, light. When he threw his shovel aside and approached her, Janice whacked the light, shattering it, and the pit went black. As Big Jack stuck out his arms, groped and grabbed, she flailed at him, kicked him, clawed and crawled under him as his arms waved around in the pitch dark. That's when she started talking to him: about her dreams mostly, how she wanted to get married and have kids, but first she wanted to help her pa and pay his hospital bills. She wanted to get her sister off meth and take care of her kids, buy them clothes. She wanted to fix the house up, sign up for the nursing program at the local college, keep paying her new truck off so she could establish credit. . . . And as she spoke, she realized that Big Jack was less and less intent on grabbing her and raping her.

He paused, huffing to ask questions of her. "You think you can make it in school? When I was a boy, every morning my momma tucked my shirt in my jeans and kissed me, telling me I was the best-looking kid in the world, and I believed her. When she said that to me, I felt like I was the cutest and most best-looking boy ever born, and I walked tall and I helped other kids, since I was so strong and I wanted to do good, and I did. I helped ladies cross the streets, I flagged the bus down and helped kids get on board, I visited old men and women and sick kids in the hospital and brought them chocolates.

"Then the day came when I was in class and this girl in the back was sending a note to her friend up front . . . the kid behind me passed it to me, and I was supposed to pass it on, but I didn't. I opened it and read it. It was a list written by the back girl answering the front girl. On that list were the names of boys, ranked most handsome to the ugliest, and both girls agreed on the ugliest. . . . My name was at the bottom.

"My mother had been lying to me to the whole time. I went to the bathroom during class and stared at myself in the mirror. My face was full of pock marks, my ears were too big, my nose was too fleshy, my lips chapped easy, my eyes were too large, my head was a big ball full of nothin' but ugly. I was ugly. I went to the playground for recess, and that was when I beat up my first kid with a stick, bloodied him good, too. Next day, I beat another kid up with a rock. I knew every last one of them had been mocking me, laughing at my ugliness, talking shit about my looks."

The machines in the mill droned above and under Big Jack's voice, a monotone rumble that vibrated throughout the steel structure. Janice could feel the rumble in the concrete and in the air of the massive machines giving shape to molten steel as it cooled to harden. Above the din, she told Jack how one of the plant guards had vandalized her pickup. Her truck was everything to her. Big Jack knew what she meant, because his truck was his most valuable possession.

"When I first started at the mill," Jack said, "some men jumped me and emptied my wallet. Up on the second floor, where daylight don't reach . . . all dust and shadows up there. Them windows ain't windows, they're walls of caked red . . . dust-dirt. Back then, I did the shittiest jobs, up by the smokestacks, and started feeling myself something like that hunchback dude in the movies, you know, someone that hides 'cause he's too ugly. Didn't help that by then I got uglier. . . . Had my ear bitten off by a bunch of Dagos, had my nose broken a dozen times in barroom brawls, teeth cracked and chipped so bad I had to cap 'em all with silver. I scared people. I liked working in the basement, liked those furnaces and stacks and shoveling that red dust and pushing the wheelbarrow and dumping it in that box. By the end of my shift, I was covered in red dust . . . took away some of my ugliness, made me look red, and you couldn't see these holes in my face."

Janice heard horns blowing, felt the vibration of overhead cranes moving tons of coils and tractors thudding concrete with loads of scrap iron and sheets of steel. Even if she screamed as loud as she could, no one would hear her. She'd just pissed off Big Jack.

"Jack, just like you, lotsa people feel like they don't belong. I party with 'em, I smoke joints alongside 'em at break time, and they tell me terrible stories of other women, the ones before me, what they did to them, and that I couldn't—no—wouldn't let them do to me. They get pregnant, and it's over. Hell, half the women workin' here are pregnant and still do twice the work as a man for half the pay. When I came in, I was only seventeen. I lied about my age to get in."

Big Jack was breathing hard in the dark. "You know, I never been part of anything here except work. No baseball teams, no pool team, no bowling, no nothing. Sometimes, I go up on the roof and I can see the whole town from up there at night . . . shines like a city in a dream. I grab that railing wishing I could be part of something."

"You know, Jack, in the locker room . . . I hear almost every woman is divorced or having an affair with someone in the mill. It's like workers become more family than family at home. They invite me to Halloween and Christmas parties, but I never go. They wanna get high and fuck, and I got better things to do, bigger things on my mind, like school."

"Used to be," Jack said, "you'd hear an ambulance siren at least once a day come in here. I don't understand why you'd wanna work here."

"I needed a job, and sometimes a person will do anything to get one and then do anything to keep it. But I ain't getting myself raped, ain't allowing that no way, no how. Ya hear me, Jack?"

"Been happening for years, long before you were born. It's how a woman gets on in the mill. Fucking and getting fucked."

"Not to this one it ain't."

A short while later, Janice and Big Jack walked out of that pit holding hands, much to the shock of every worker in the plant. She'd never explain to them what went on or how she got him to change his mind, but she told me as much as she'd ever let on to anyone.

"You see, when I broke that light bulb, everything was pitch black. I couldn't see Big Jack, and more importantly, he couldn't see me. We had no bodies, no flesh, no hair or eyes, only voices. We were two spirits talking, two souls sharing dreams and worries. We were just two souls in the dark, like children, whispering with our voices that were spirits . . . not bodies, spirits."

And the more I thought about it, she had something there. I mean, take away our bodies and colors and genders, no sex, and you have spirits. I never heard of a spirit yelling at another spirit, "You don't belong, you're a foreigner," or a spirit getting beat up because of the color of its skin or culture.

PREDATOR

I had moved into my place, and to be honest I was feeling more Christmassy than I've ever felt. I mean, no matter how hard you try, being in LA for Christmas is not exactly Christmas. Colorado with its snowy mountains? New Mexico with its traditional *luminarias* and nativity scenes in yards and parades and snow? Yep. But LA? A million ornaments, ribbons on the lamp posts with green, silver and red bunting, skyscraper candles and hot air balloon-sized Santas on rooftops just don't make it.

I was all set for my first Christmas back in Santa Luz, looking out the window as snowflakes sealed the land in sweet innocence. Sheryl, an old friend, and her husband Jason, who I didn't know, and their kids were coming over to share a Christmas meal with me. I was looking forward to seeing her again. Apron on, oven warming my kitchen, I made us green chili stew, lamb chops, tortillas, corn and beans.

Sheryl and Jason were up in Colorado, heading down to Santa Luz on the evening of December 23rd. They were driving back from a holiday party at Jason's friend's house in southern Colorado, heading toward Taos, then to Santa Luz. The roads were snow-packed and slick with ice and getting more so as they climbed the lower foothills toward Piedra Azul.

I could imagine how they were feeling good about having visited their friends. Sheryl was a social being who loved people, but from what I heard from some of the people at the party, Sheryl was annoyed at Jason's flirting. In emails she'd told me he'd been that way with his first marriage and, now that he worked as a trainer at a gym, it had gotten worse. He'd bulked up with heavy weight training and a dozen different protein shakes. He had shaved every follicle of hair from his body, strained the budget to buy special lotions, vitamins, colognes, new clothes and hair tonics. Now, he strutted about the house like a gamecock. This didn't bother her as much as the secret phone calls and the late-night outings supposedly to see a friend who needed his help. Sometimes she would call me in the middle of the night. There were the excuses for not having shown up at her law office for a party to celebrate a successful defense case. He also stayed up at night emailing people he claimed were clients. And then, there were those women at the gym who constantly stopped him to talk when she was there. She knew in her heart what was going on.

Sheryl had graduated from law school, was busting her ass working twelve-hour days and had gained a lot of weight. She wasn't looking as good as when she was seventeen and had met Jason. I knew then that she was crazy about him even though I warned her that he was a liar—not that I knew first-hand from experience, but I sensed it. And I listened to my gut.

I knew her well. We'd been friends since childhood. But I guess I didn't know her that well. I could see Sheryl, focused on the road, buzzed and nursing more than a little resentment at him, aggravated by his disappearing for thirty minutes during the visit with Mabel and her husband. From her emails and texts, Sheryl and Jason had talked about splitting up, but she knew he needed her—she was making the money, he was fucking the girls. She paid all the bills, right down to the vitamin gummy bears and juice boxes for their two kids. He kept telling her he was trying to talk sense to her, explain the futility of keeping him against his wishes, that they would remain friends, that she couldn't keep him against his will. It was wrong.

I, too, would tell her to leave him, to come out to LA and stay with me. I had an extra room and the beach was only a few blocks away; she and the kids would love it. But she said she couldn't miss work.

Jason's arguments went nowhere. Sheryl knew the law and she'd pillage his ass if he ever tried to abandon her. He feared that, feared she'd obliterate him. If he wanted to wipe the slate clean, that slate would be smeared with his blood.

Earlier in the evening, when they had started back, he promised they'd be together forever, vowing to end his life if she left. It was guilt and sheer gibberish. He plotted, he conspired, he lied, confusing her. Over time, however, she grew to understand his clever hustle: keep her on a leash, always dangling the possibility of withdrawing his affection. He could be cruel, even violent, commanding. Shoes had to be lined up by the door, the house cleaned, the dishes washed, the laundry done, while he was off with friends, women, parading around all of them like he had the world by the balls and nothing could harm him. He was immune from worry, and when he wanted something, he'd do anything to get his way, even force her to believe his lies, persuade her that he was innocent when she knew in her gut he was a betraying sack of shit. How long could she go on? She didn't know. She was weary, broken down, hopeless. One thing was certain, he had a hold on her. He was good at keeping her, good at strategizing his power over her. She gave in, feeling helpless and fatigued by the constant suspicions assailing her. She told herself she just didn't care anymore. But she did.

Her maternal instinct reasoned that no matter what, the kids should not be traumatized. Sheryl stubbornly refused to even consider leaving, even though she probably would have done just fine on her own. It was the lingering vestiges of her youthful stupidity still bubbling in her brain, thinking she was so lucky to have such a handsome man. That's what he always told her, and she was sufficiently brainwashed.

Marooned, I think. That's what I feel.

This is just your pit stop, hey, not an end destination.

And I'm desperate for rescue with no mainland in sight.

A wall was being erected and rising higher every day between us, topped with bitter remarks and angry glass shards and barbwire accusations and lies as to make it impossible to breach. But there is a way to get over it, fly over . . .

∽ ∾

Jason was a courteous go-getter, preening himself to go to the gym each morning. Good-looking, and working with the prettiest girls, embracing them from behind when showing them how to use weights, holding their waists and touching their bellies and arms when he guided them on the elliptical machine, touching their feet and thighs on the stationary bicycle under the guise of good posture, sitting next to them on the yoga mats and stretching with them, all the while pretending to help them while getting them turned on. He was deliberate, and to his mind, the dumb bitches went for it. They were like her, working and lonely and abused.

If she could only rewind to the moment when they were in love . . . how they played in bed for hours, her body tight and firm and youthful. He'd chase her across the park, laughing, on summer afternoons. They'd sit on the grass near the taco wagon, eat their tacos and drink Mexican bottled Coke and then play cards under the concrete umbrellas surrounding the tennis courts. They'd watch the families go by and they'd plan their own future family.

I thank the Creator for the gift of tears, because without being able to cry I don't know what would have become of me. My sadness. I don't want our daughters to grow up like him, lying and cheating and seeing me cry all the time because of his betrayals.

I will write our story now, the ending at least . . .

I don't need to recall the exact time or situation, or the people or place, when something in me broke. Time flies through my pores and traverses the terrain of my experiences. I learned that

love always comes with a dual edge—we have our public per-
sonae where we get along and smile and picnic with the colleagues, and then the ones we preserve for our private
lives—crying in a dark bedroom waiting for him to come home.
Smelling perfume on him. Even his cock smelled of other vaginas.

When he forced me to masturbate him, my fingers felt
scalded. Coming in my mouth, taking me from behind, the whole
time my mind kept searching for a way to escape—one part of my
mind justifying it as a game lovers play and the other part as an
evil initiation into compliance with dark forces that unsettled me
to the very core of my heart.

It wasn't anything so occult as that. Pretty basic stuff. After
he had gone to "work," probably to meet one of his women, I'd
fill the sink and disinfect the whips and lotion bottles and dildos.
They cost a lot of money, you know.

He likes it when I call him master. He makes me kneel . . . get
on my back and spread my legs high so he can enter me from behind, looking into my face. I guess it was that word, master, that
got to me more than anything: calling him master. The tone of his
voice scares the shit out of me, and during those times it seems I
cross an invisible line from which there is no going back.

A rash of regret that I am leaving spreads over me. It's an
awful feeling. The way Buddhists in a temple spend weeks sifting
colored sand to draw a mandala, painstakingly finger-praying
each sand grain into its place only to sweep it away—that's our
days, blue and red sand blowing in the moonlight. Except that
for Jason and me, there are no prayers, no ancient rituals that
consecrate our ruin, nothing between him and me and the destruction of our days, of the people in them, of the hopes and
dreams we had mashed by the cloven demon of betrayal. No separation distances us from the night's collapse. I drag myself in
ash-coloured grief, surrender to eternal sleep, cowering with fear
of what might come.

I've decided to confront him head-on. Barns, haystacks, dogs, trucks and tractors—even lights inside houses all seem so . . . so innocent and ordinary.

It's getting late and I have to leave.

I glance in the rearview mirror at our sweet girls sleeping.

◦◦ ◦◦

Sheryl drove up the mountain road until it leveled off at the Rio Grande Gorge. Her headlights caught the curve ahead with its warning sign to slow down to 15 mph, but in bitter repudiation of all that was rational and with no small amount of self-loathing for what she had done to get into this dead-end marriage, she glanced in the rearview mirror at her two daughters, tears streaming down her cheeks as her foot pressed the gas pedal.

PLAYER

She was the first person I called when I got back to Santa Luz. When I drove into her yard and saw how the weeds had grown, just the eyesore and unruliness of all the dead grass, decrepit picket fence, stuff that neighborhood kids had thrown in like papers and cans and miniature whiskey bottles, it was depressing and worrisome. Had she gone off the deep end into drugs or booze or been inflicted with such betrayal by an ex-lover that she no longer cared about the appearance of her place? I hoped none of the above were true and was relieved when I walked in and hugged her and saw how she was still my Helen, the best friend a person could have.

It was me who recommended to Helen that she get some help from the halfway house, use those strong ex-cons to get her house in order. Helen was one of those women who worked, who helped others, who was ready at a moment's notice to serve someone in need. She was giving to a fault.

She was a drug and alcohol counselor, and helped out at Santa Ana pueblo in the greenhouse. Which made what happened all the more astonishing and bewildering.

I didn't know where any halfway houses were in Santa Luz, but Helen's neighbor suggested she call the halfway house just off Canyon Road and ask if they had anyone willing to work cleaning up her basement, patching the leaky living room ceiling and screwing in the electrical outlets sticking out from several places in the walls. The plumbers who had fixed the leaky pipes down there had made a mess and abandoned it—actually, not plumbers, but a handyman who claimed he knew all about plumbing because his uncle was one and he used to help him and, ultimately, it leaked the day after he was gone. She had fed him like a king, even went to Whole Foods (which costs her a fortune every time) and made him Armenian coffee, sandwiches with cheese, lettuce, salami—all organic, of course—for half her paycheck.

That was in good faith, of which she had little those days. So when Helen's neighbor told her about the halfway house, she was more careful. She took this fellow, Logan, to a coffee shop on Cerrillos near the halfway house and asked him questions about why he'd been in prison, where he was from and his family. "Crossing drugs through the international border from Aguas, Mexico, into . . ." She couldn't remember the name but it was famous for racing ducks. Duck races—what next, right? He was from this duck town. He said his son died while he was in prison. His father was a hired day laborer and had his son with him one afternoon when he was pitchforking hay to the cows on a ranch. The boy died of asphyxiation—he was allergic to the hay dust. Asthmatic, she guessed, feeling sad about the situation. His wife had left him. Pretty much everything he attempted in life he failed at. Out of pity, she hired him. (It was one of those situations you see happening right before your eyes. You say nothing and much later you find yourself regretting it because you know you should have said *something*.)

Pity or no pity, her oldest son wasn't going for it. After Josh went downstairs to meet Logan, he came right back up and demanded she get rid of him.

"Mom, he's a thug, he's going to rob you blind or worse. You can see it, the man's a con artist!"

Other friends reacted in the same way, warning her, "His tattoos, Helen, they're all over him. . . . He's in a gang, he's dangerous, please be careful."

She dismissed them all, didn't expect anything less from them: painters, sculptors, performance artists, weavers, poets. She had run a gallery down in the plaza, and they were all clients of hers. They were the pure ones, the ones who never got their hands dirty, the ones who aired their grievances the way artists do, with their chins up in arrogant superiority, as if expecting anyone else to do their dirty work, as long as they didn't have to break a sweat doing what they called "menial work."

Despite their misgivings, she and Logan became friends, even dated. Maybe she did it to spite them, to rub it in their face. She told herself, rather smugly, that she was above this stereotyping; she didn't need to scapegoat to feel worthier or more ethical. They could censor him and criticize all they wanted. She knew to her mind and body it was a simple case of attraction. He made her feel hot, gave her body goosebumps, got her wet just thinking about him at night when she was in bed.

She had not dated in a long time. A middle-aged white woman who frequented the gym and compared her sagging boobs and wobbly thighs and facial jowls and—stop there, she didn't need to crucify herself. Yes, she was getting old and needed a little love, a little "upliftment" from the daily boredom of her life.

He wasn't handsome or charming or intelligent—a mother would be hard-pressed not to abandon such a ferret-looking creature. But his one saving grace, and she dared say it, even in his deeply ingrained proclivity toward criminal enterprise, was his humor.

She had always been a sucker for humor. Anyone who could make her laugh had her in bed naked and waiting with open legs. He must have sensed her weakness. Every time he made snipping comments at people, he had her belly aching and muffling her mouth with her hand, if not downright peeing her undies.

He convinced her to rent him an apartment, also to put a down payment on a '91 250 Ford truck, lend him money and buy him an iPhone. She did all the above, laughing her way into bed and increasing poverty.

Then one night, Helen's cell rang. When she answered it, she realized it was a pocket call but didn't hang up. She heard a strange voice talking to a woman, cursing and telling her, "Sell the drugs. . . . Get out on the plaza early and sell that ass to the tourists. I need the fuckin' money."

The gruff voice continued, "We kin grab a shitload a money . . . just get yer friends over and push that meth . . . pull in that cash. Now!"

A day or so later, her cell rang and she answered only to hear the sad sound of someone walking in the summer afternoon heat on gravel. She recognized the heavy rhythmic pace of the footsteps—crunch-crunch-crunch—and the labored dry breathing that meant the walker was a smoker. The sound of it made her think of a lonely man looking for a job, a walk of despair, of someone who had no purpose in life.

Helen was forty-eight, a single Jewish woman trying to find a good man with more than a one-night stand for brains. Somehow Logan knew from her first words that she was lonely in a way that sometimes compromises a woman's deepest standards and lowers them to depths she would never have imagined.

One night, Logan showed up with a small palm-sized scale and a nugget of something that looked like a diamond.

"What's this?" she asked.

As charming as ever, as if he had just handed her an invitation to attend a black-tie garden party, Logan said, "It's for you . . . it's meth. And a scale to weigh it."

Rarely was Helen at a loss for words but she truly did not know what to say. The only thing she could think to do was to reach above the kitchen counter into the cupboard and set the rock aside. As Logan turned and went out to continue pulling weeds, Helen wondered what she had just done.

It wasn't long before she found herself puffing it with him, just to try it and see what it was like. No doubt, it was a miracle drug for intercourse. They fucked all night and into the next day. Helen slept eleven hours straight. When she finally got up, she went to the cupboard, pulled out the remaining meth, tossed it into the toilet and flushed.

When Logan arrived to work out in the yard, she handed him his scale and said, "I don't want it."

"Well, then, you can at least do me a favor . . . one last thing to help me get me on my feet. . . . I promise, I'll never bother you again. I'll move back home and get a job and take care of my parents."

She did care for him, and out of a sense of empathy she agreed to try and help him.

"Can you ask your friends if they'd like to buy some," he asked sheepishly, "and I'll do the selling . . . just one time, that's all."

And so she did. Helen did not see any harm in asking them, and to her surprise almost all her artist friends were willing to pool their money together for a large amount that they could divvy up and use over a period of a year or so.

Three of her friends had scrounged enough money together to buy an ounce of meth and use it in a hotel suite for the night. After having a few drinks in the hotel bar, Helen and Logan joined them in their suite. All Helen could think of was getting the deal done and them leaving. But soon, she found herself taking a puff of the meth pipe and then feeling horny.

Helen drank heavily, and time flew by while she was high. Before she knew it, she could see the pale rose color of dawn on the horizon, and with the dawn light, some friends of Logan joined the party. They immediately started in snorting, drinking and bullshitting. A girl was sitting in a big La-Z-Boy reading a book of poetry while her boyfriend was jabbering on about the coke business with Logan. Three other friends, who were buzzed to the hilt and enjoying themselves as if these last few hours were all they had on earth, laughed and laughed at Logan's jokes.

One couple said they were from Chicago and that they hadn't slept in days. It was obvious, as the boyfriend kept jumping up and down, walking around and sputtering half phrases to himself; he'd calm down and then go full tilt again babbling about something or other.

Around noon, the girl suddenly set the book down on her lap, turned to her boyfriend and blurted out, "Go to hell, you abuser! I'm not doing a thing you say from now on. I'm tired of your shit."

Everyone looked at each other, confused and apprehensive. The last thing anyone wanted to do was mess with the dude's head when he was squirmy. An obvious methhead on a week of no sleep could be unpredictable and dangerous, and Helen knew it. She saw him give his girlfriend a crazy stare and run outside. She realized they were in trouble.

He returned carrying a sawed-off shotgun, grabbed his girl by the neck and shoved her to the floor.

"Oh, yeah," he screamed, "I'll show you what you're going to do."

The mad tweaker, looming over her, placed the shotgun at her mouth and yelled, "I'll kill you!"

Helen threw a hard look at Logan as if to beg him to intervene. Half the hotel rooms were filled with partiers, and it was even rumored downstairs in the casino lobby that the governor was partying in one of them, but for Helen, what seemed like an ordinary party suddenly turned into a possible murder scene.

And what did jocular Logan do? Instead of confronting the gunman, he skulked into the bathroom.

Not knowing what to do but knowing she had to do something, Helen stood up, went up to the guy and said, "Hey, buddy, ease up . . . just chill. Everything is okay."

Bad move.

He turned his bloodshot eyes with sleepless rage onto Helen and shoved the double-barreled end of the rifle between her legs and pressed it against her vagina.

"You little bitch," he spat out. "What d'ya think you're going to do about it?"

He backed her up, shoving the barrel against her sex harder, until she was pressed against the wall next to the bedroom door.

"What d'ya think now, huh? What d'ya think?" he screamed.

The girl on the floor rose on one elbow, leaned toward her boyfriend and growled, "Kill her, baby, kill her! Kill that piece of shit."

Helen's heart slapped against her rib cage, faster and faster, and she knew she was having a heart attack. All she could think of was to slow her heart down. "Slow down, slow down," she forced herself to think.

He turned back to his girl, hit her with the butt of the shotgun and then smacked her with his hand a few times, yelling "Who now? Who's going to do what I tell them? . . . You, you are!"

Helen took his momentary distraction as an opportunity to get away. She opened the bedroom door, went in quietly and locked it behind her. As silently as she could, she got on the bed and whispered to herself, "Breathe . . . breathe . . . breathe." She took deep swallows of air, inhaled and exhaled slowly, repeating, "Slow . . . slow down . . . slow down," drawing longer breaths until her heart started easing back.

The whole time she was bringing her heart palpitations down, she could hear the methhead screaming in the other room, whipped up into a frenzy about who was a man and who wasn't. Just as her heart finally calmed enough, she heard five shots roar out and a door slam. It was not until an hour later or more that she had the courage to rise. She got to her feet quietly, took the screen off the window, climbed out onto the balcony, down a trellis and got into her car. Helen hit the access road and then took a left onto I-40. She passed a bait shop and a billboard with a cabin on it, announcing to motorists, "Come relax, you deserve it."

Her mind was blank, her body numb. Later that day, she answered the doorbell and was confronted with police cars in her driveway and two detectives ordering her to turn around. She was being charged with four counts of first-degree murder. That's when she called me. I went down to the station and she told me what happened. Wow, I thought to myself, leaving LA I had the feeling I was brushing off the crime crap that plagues big cities and held the naïve assumption that Santa Luz would be calm and nourishing. Boy, was I wrong.

SWEENEY'S LAST SUPPER

It's a strange thing to think you know someone and then bam, he strips away the outer covering, tears away the mask and appears as he really is. It leaves you stunned, immobile, helpless, wondering what is going on in this world. An ebullient, socially engaging man with a big, hearty smile turns into a freak right before your disbelieving eyes. This was Paul Sweeney, a husky Irish fellow married to a Jewish lawyer, the father of a lovely daughter and an intelligent son on his way to the university.

When I returned to Santa Luz, Paul invited me to the high school to speak in his son's class about the movies and writing screenplays. The night before there'd been a shooting not far from my house, and I mentioned this to him when he picked me up. He thought I was making it up. I showed him where the shooting had taken place—there was still blood on the street. He didn't seem surprised, just commented that the whole damn city was being run by the cartels out of Juarez. "Meth," he repeated, "meth is the new king."

It frightened me enough so I couldn't get back to sleep or think coherently. When I stood before the class, I rambled on, spouting nonsense. I was glad when I finished, and afterwards I hit he gym and lifted weights to try and get the unease out of my body. On my way out I stopped at the announcement board and read a flyer of some people asking for help picking up needles that junkies were throwing in parks and driveways. Apparently, a needle had stuck a little girl in one of the parks as she was playing.

I answered the ad and volunteered. They coupled me with Mrs. Chávez, who came out every morning and picked up the needles that junkies had thrown in her driveway. She lived in a respectable Santa Luz neighborhood. Her home, or as she called it, "the family home," had been passed down several generations, and now she was in charge of taking care of it. As she swept up the syringes, she thought of the poor people who needed to stick those ugly things into their bodies. "They must have terrible problems," she said to me one morning. "I mean, a human being stabbing himself in the veins with toxic chemicals so powerful that they leave the user mindless and crazed?"

Mrs. Chávez had seen a program on PBS once about some monks in yellow and burgundy robes who sat in front of other monks who stood over them cursing and screaming. The sitting monks smiled at their aggressors and, according to the narrator of the program, the monks learned to empathize with their aggressors, acknowledging that those screaming monks must have suffered tremendous emotional and spiritual pain to act with such hostile behavior.

"Poor things," was Mrs. Chávez's reaction. And now, each bloodied hypodermic needle she picked up was an angry face screaming at the world, screaming at her. Another needle, another angry face placed in her bag. She only wished she could go to all the parks and do the same.

One morning, however, when I met her for our ritual gathering of needles, Mrs. Chávez was very tired. She and her husband had driven to Farmington, in the northern part of the state, where they had attended their younger daughter's college graduation. As she stooped to pick up another needle in the driveway, her neighbors, the DeSotos, were walking their granddaughter Esmeralda, chatting and laughing, unaware of the needles. Sud-

denly, Esmeralda screamed. They looked down to see a needle
piercing her left foot.

I rushed her to the emergency room. Later that afternoon, still
at the hospital, a doctor confirmed that the needle carried the
AIDS virus. Mr. DeSoto was enraged, angry enough to pursue
help in any way he could. After taking the sad news to his daughter and son-in-law, DeSoto spent days on the computer in search
of legal aid. Finally, he was able to locate a lawyer through the
law school at the local college. A professor Rose Sweeney, Paul's
wife, volunteered to take on the case pro bono against the City of
Santa Luz Health Department and the local Needle Exchange
Program that supplied addicts with free syringes.

The Sweeneys were a good family. Paul was always willing
to help. He had a camera and would show up and video certain
programs for me. Sometimes he joined me at the gym and hit the
pool, other times we rode bikes together. I told him I really ap-
preciated what his wife was doing for the DeSotos, how much I
wanted to find the dirty culprit responsible for spreading terror in
the neighborhood parks. I shared with him how I had called the
city hall and begged them to install cameras so we might catch the
drug fiend and how I was summarily dismissed. They said if I
wanted cameras, then I should install them myself. I called Mayor
Keller's office to see if they might send a crew down to help clean
up the park, and I was ignored again. I had assumed they were
there in office to help us citizens, but they acted like we were enemies, hostiles in enemy territory.

Sweeney's wife came through for me, though. Rose worked
with a private investigator, Dan White, who would follow the trail
of the needle to and from the Needle Exchange. He'd find out
who had received it and used it and how they had disposed of it
in Mrs. Chávez's driveway.

As it turned out, Paul actually volunteered at the Needle Exchange. He declared that he wanted to find the person responsible but not at the cost of closing down the program that was the

only one in town to help addicts. As I said, they were a compassionate family, and I had to agree with him. I didn't want to see the program closed down.

Paul cautioned the DeSotos about suing the Exchange, because if the suit were successful and the program shut down, many people could die from using infected needles. But Rose saw no other alternative. She had to bring attention to the problem. It was an epidemic in Santa Luz: all the parks were littered with needles, the city's concrete channels were filled with addicts. She had to demand that the city council and health agencies provide a remedy . . . or other innocent children would keep getting infected with AIDS and other diseases. Anyone playing barefooted in the parks could be pricked, even pets. And the elderly who frequently walked in slippers would be at risk.

Rose Sweeney pursued the case. Investigator Dan White developed his leads and her husband Paul alerted all his clients in the homeless camps and under city bridges to stop tossing syringes into the parks and people's yards and driveways. It could have caused serious strife in the Sweeney household, but Paul eventually understood that Rose had an obligation to represent the DeSoto child. He honored his commitment to the intravenous users by warning them to be more conscientious about where they discarded their needles.

৩৯ ৩৯

Paul Sweeney dressed to the nines. No . . . better than that. He was a walking, talking stack of thousand-dollar casino chips, and life was a green felt card table in a by-invitation-only backroom poker game. He was overwhelmingly charming, had a brilliant mind, a disarming smile and a pair of blue eyes that twinkled. But that smile . . . that smile made the receiver feel he was the only one in the world and lucky to have Paul Sweeney as his friend.

He seemed infallible and could do no wrong, although very few people knew what he did all day. Stories floated around that he'd been a serious heroin addict at one time, a meth abuser, a cokehead, but since he kept his private life closed to scrutiny, no one really knew him or his history. At odd times during the day he'd stop by my house to say hi and chat. I never thought anything odd about it. His wife worked so he could take his daughter to private school miles away by the foothills and then pick her up. He was charged with caring for the kids. Considering that his wife taught law all day, it was a reasonable arrangement. Some said he worked for the police as an undercover narc; others swore they'd seen him with women, some underage girls, some as young as 14 and 15. When they looked at him, they often saw bags under his eyes; his blue eyes concealed as much as they revealed. People often noticed a furtive glance, a gleam in the blue eye that made them nervous. It left them feeling they didn't want to know more about him, that nodding at him when they passed was enough—anything further would certainly reveal danger.

He spent his days going to the gym and driving around in his new car. He was known for his shiny black suit and an Irish lilt that transported the listener to a bucolic hillside with sheep and sheep dogs and surf banging against cliffs as depicted on postcards of Ireland, land of the poets. He was well read and could recite poems from memory, but somehow after meeting him, people were left with some apprehension. He left a particular sting in the air. There was, all in all, a certain guardedness that accompanied his inveterate joviality.

It bothered him greatly that Mr. DeSoto's suit could shut down the Needle Exchange centers and endanger so many junkies' lives. For once, he was stumped, not knowing how to halt the attack on his cherished centers or his unfortunate clients. He'd been handing out needles for so long that he couldn't remember when he didn't, and there was no way he was going to allow old man DeSoto to destroy the good work he and a dozen other volunteers were doing in the city of Santa Luz, which was infested with meth, heroin and wealthy coke addicts. If there was one thing he had learned being married to an excellent lawyer, it was the value and importance of research. In particular, he came to understand that every single person had something to hide. He would find out what secrets DeSoto was hiding. Once discovered, he'd warn Desoto to withdraw his suit or face his secrets being revealed to the public and his reputation being destroyed. It did not matter that DeSoto was considered by all his neighbors to be a very good and trustworthy man.

It was wrong to blackmail DeSoto, Sweeney accepted that, but it had to be done. Harsh means were needed for immediate results. So, for the next few months, starting in August, at the city library, Paul scoured the Internet, searching back into DeSoto's past. By the beginning of December, he was convinced he had enough to paint an unsavory picture of DeSoto, albeit nothing serious enough to warrant notifying the authorities

Sweeney sent his first email, signed "John Smyth," from an internet café frequented by skateboarders, graffiti artists, goth gangs and grungers. It did not have the effect Sweeney had hoped for. DeSoto shot back that he thought Sweeney was a predator and a coward. This in turn provoked Sweeney to write two raging emails that accused DeSoto of abuses that were actually committed by another person with the same last name:

1. The pervasive abuse from you towards me and many others is something that you've psychologically become habituated to. It must stop. I was really looking forward to you reporting me to someone: the police, APD, DEA, whatever institution you could think up. It's extremely disappointing that you haven't. I do not have a decent thing to say about you because everything you say or do is always predicated by some type of deceitfulness. You are the consummate snake in the

grass. You are a serial abuser, liar, and cocaine and street methamphetamine user.

2. I know you attacked a child abuser/rapist in his own home and killed him in the toilet with a shower curtain. Here is a list of the people you have exploited over the last thirty years . . . since 1998. Me, Benny, Jaime, Maria, Valentino and many others. You didn't pay them for work, you accused them of drug abuse, you reported them for stealing stuff . . . all of this readily available down at the City Hall complaints department.

In a third email, he wrote:

We have not hurt you. By we, I mean needle users. And yet you want to shut down our centers. You are a man without integrity. You have no life but to hustle and make others miserable. I'm sick of you. The mere mention of your name makes me want to puke. I have no pity nor sympathy for you.

When Mr. DeSoto emailed him back, stating he had no idea what he was talking about, Paul Sweeney went into a frenzy:

Listen fucker, I'm just as pissed off at you since you began falsely accusing me of stupid fuckin nonsense. Prick up your ears and listen one more and final time, because you will never hear from me again. You are a no good using cunt that gets away with a lot of shit. You've fucked over a lot of people and made a shitload of enemies. And there's no amount of atoning for that shit. Needles, break-ins, lawn mower thefts . . . Make no mistake, let me make it perfectly clear, I have enough anger to . . . Yeah, yeah, you piss me off, but I'm not really all that angry, cause you're dying first. Get it, asshole?

Paul Sweeney

Mr. DeSoto decided not to respond. This Paul Sweeney character was way out there orbiting in his own dark, addict universe.
He thought about what to do with the threats from a man who
seemed totally rocking mad. One thing was for certain: the suit
was doing its work. DeSoto decided to recede into the background and let the justice system do its work.

Another email arrived, short but menacing:

Your heart is as blackened and maggot ridden as the
foulest on earth. What a fuckin motherfucker you are.
What an asshole. What a fraud. What a faker.

Who supports you in your suit? No one, because you
have no one. You're a depressed, lonely old cunt who's
about to die. If you don't stop bothering us with your shit,
then you'll feel my real wrath. I'll be the one fucking
your cunt face.

ഹ ൟ

Two weeks before the case was to be heard, Rose Sweeney
decided she needed a break and she accepted her friend's offer to
go for a long hike that weekend. They went into the Santa Fe Forest and stopped to picnic and talk. Her friend plucked a tiny red
mushroom no bigger than her thumbnail and warned her to never
eat that type because it was highly toxic. Rose plucked another
and secured it in a sandwich baggie to save to show her kids and
warn them about never eating one.

The same weekend Rose Sweeney had gone hiking, Dan
White dropped off his findings in a folder and placed it on her
desk, but she didn't get it until two days before they were supposed to go to court. She had somehow buried it under other paperwork and just had enough time to quickly read the nine pages
of double-spaced assessments and leaf through the accompany-
ing photos and summary. Something in them made her blanch,

something so important that when she went to court and the pro-
ceedings started, she was called before the judge. She had to stand
there in front of the packed courtroom and be scolded for not including the necessary paperwork. The judge threw the case out
with a warning to her and her fellow colleagues, who were all
just as shocked if not more at her grievous oversight. It was unlike her. Very unlike her.

Paul Sweeney had never seen his wife so distraught. To cheer
her up, he offered to go to Whole Foods and buy the best tilapia
and wine and French bread. Of course, she had to cook it all up.
That evening when he came home from the gym, she was already
preparing the feast.

He assumed it was a good thing, since it had taken her out of
her morose mood. She was finally emerging from her silent co-
coon of disappointment. He set the table, chattered away affably
about coaching the girls' soccer team, about someone he met at
the gym, about new policies being implemented at the Needle
Exchange to ensure no needles were tossed in neighborhood
yards. . . . There he was, clearing the table and washing the dishes,
an *Esquire* model: blond hair with lumberjack handsomeness,
masculine square chin, blue eyes that beamed with merriment.
He feigned interest in whatever she said, as if Rose were the most
important and interesting woman he'd ever heard. He laughed,
joked, always on-call with his generosity and kindness and readi-
ness to spin a tale for her.

That evening, hours after dinner, Rose Sweeney gave the following testimony to a police detective:

"On the night in question when I got home, my husband
made a delicious plate of blue-corn enchiladas. Perhaps this special dinner was because I knew and, knowing what I knew, knowing he was leaving forever, he was a bit nostalgic.

"He loved fish enchiladas and he made them so good. He
scraped the plate with the last bit of tortilla and then went to bed
all full and content and happy as a pig in mud. Except hours later,

he woke up from a dead sleep, drenched in sweat and writhing in excruciating pain. He rolled off the bed onto the floor and called me. I went and stood over him as he grabbed his mid-section, rocking and holding his stomach in a fetal position. Tears rolled down his cheeks. He begged me to get him to the hospital.

"That's when I threw the folder at him, the one my private investigator Dan White gave me with a photo of him getting his dick sucked in a car by the park. There was another photo of him shooting up with some derelict junkies under a freeway pass . . . and another of him in the back seat fucking some underage girl in front of Mr. Chávez's house and later tossing needles in his driveway.

"I stood still as a statue a few feet from him, imagining that little red mushroom making its way to his heart like a red June bug. He had an expression on his face like he was hypnotized, as if he was absolutely unaware of me. I remained frozen to his outstretched arms, stared down at him and contemplated whether I should let him die or not. I can only imagine what he saw in me at that moment, in my face. . . .

"He begged me to please get the keys and start the car and get him to the hospital. He was sweating all over, and his pain was overwhelming: 'Like a pair of hot scissors is slashing away at my stomach lining,' he said.

"I finally moved to get the keys, helped him up off the floor and out to the car . . . and to the hospital.

"He woke up days later with the doctor asking him when was the last time he had visited a forest and whether he had eaten mushrooms . . . the poisonous kind.

"'Never,' he replied, and he insisted that the only way he could contract such a lethal dose of the poison was if someone had poisoned him. Of course, that led to me.

"A bag was attached to the bed frame and a tube ran into his side where they drained a green fluid for days. After a couple of days, he began to sit up and even started tottering up and down the corridor, lumbering one slippered foot in front of the other, holding his side where the green liquid was still being drained from his body."

Rose Sweeney could not follow through on her murderous plan. She saved Paul Sweeney's life. Nevertheless, something happened that we're all still trying to figure out. I hadn't seen him in a while and I knew none of what had transpired concerning him and his wife and the pictures and such, only that he was absent. I went to his house to invite him out to the gym with me. I hadn't seen him in a long time and he used to go to the gym frequently.

His house was empty; no furniture, nothing, the yard unkempt. It felt cursed, like something evil had happened there. The faint smell of blood lingered on surfaces, caught like an invisible stench on solid structures. A lingering shadow of a bad omen traced the air with ominous menace.

I was eating at Blue's when I ran into a friend of Paul's. When I asked about him about Paul, all his friend kept repeating was, "He's gone down. He's gone down. Man," shaking his head with eyes downward, "man, he's gone, man."

He didn't mean dead. He meant, as I learned later, that worse than being murdered by his wife, he had lost his wife and kids and home. His family had moved to DC to live with her parents.

These days when I'm out and about on my way from the gym or to pick up carryout, mostly riding my bike along the concrete bike paths that run parallel to the channels, I'll catch a glimpse of Paul, almost unrecognizable in rags, skin and bones, looking like he's aged fifty years. He's running with a homeless gang of meth tweakers, enduring a fate worse than being murdered. Had I been able to foresee this end, the consequence of him leading two lives, I would have intervened and done something. But in Santa Luz, things are not always what they seem, and so many peoples' faces carry a vestige of regret etched into their features. One would characterize it as a look of sorrow or long suffering, but it's regret for something that happened in their lives, a burden they must carry even as those they love are swallowed by the darkness and roam like discontented cursed souls among the armies of the night.

THE WELL

(with apologies to Guillermo del Toro)

"The Huichol dancer talks to you inside your mind." That's what her father, a scientist working at Los Alamos, told her. Ever since he said that, Maya had been trying to figure out what he meant. There was a painting her father bought from a Chicano artist during the annual artist fair held in the Santa Luz plaza, and the artist told her father, "He's a Huichol pole dancer, what they call a *volador*, from the Yucatan, and he stands on one foot on top of the pole cradling in his hands a small box. You must guess what he holds so motherly, protecting it with his hands and huddling his torso over it as if it were the most important thing in life. What is in the box? You have to guess what the sun gave him."

Her father hung the painting on the staircase wall, and every time she walked up, she paused in front of it. This was before my time, I knew her mother way before Maya was born, even before Evelina got married, pregnant and had Maya.

Maya and I met when she took a writing class from me. Her black hair, I swear, if you grabbed a handful and weighed it on a normal gym scale, it would weigh a few pounds. Thick, jet-black pueblo Indian/Chicana hair. She was wild back then, riding me hard at my apartment, slapping my thighs as if she were whipping a horse's flanks to run faster, gasping in her Indio-Chicana language *Ya-chi-chiyaa!* And me below watching her brown tits with purple nipples slap up and down, my hands on her hips and waist pushing her down hard on me, her thick mane of black hair flailing to both sides as if hurricane force winds were blowing and she was riding a bronc.

Then a lot of time passed until that afternoon in Taos at the Mabel Dodge classroom where I was holding a writing workshop, and in she walked, her row of teeth so white and strong that if only I saw that I'd know who they belonged to. She gave me the biggest smile. Her brown face and black eyebrows and bright smile and dark, dark brown eyes, black almost—all of it converged into a welcoming I-love-you.

That day, in that classroom, when I mentioned to her how I remembered her, so defiant and classy a warrior woman, so take-no-shit from any white boy, a hard gangsta poet, a pueblo poet whose father was a Chicano from LA and her mother a San Felipe pueblo woman, she cried.

Not the kind of cry you would think. No, it came on suddenly like a rare clay vessel accidentally hit and knocked to the floor and shattering—a hard self-shattering *what have I done to my life* cry, a *what has my life turned into* cry. And she stared straight at me and said, "That used to be me. Can you believe it? I married a white guy and we have a house in Santa Luz and I'm settled down now." And it was as if she was admitting to a crime, a murder, finally divulging to us where the body was buried, what weapon she used, what day and how it happened. And we all knew as we looked at her, the murdered party she was talking about was herself.

We didn't fuck that much back then, back before she was married, but enough to lead to her to believe I was her man . . . until that terrible day when we were standing under the burning afternoon sun. It was summer, she had taken me to meet her grandma and uncles and we ate and decided to go roam about the pueblo. It was feast day. Different clans were dancing. I bought

two snow cones drenched in purple syrup, and as we stood biting
into the ice chips, I told her I had to leave soon and pick up my
girlfriend at the airport. She walked away, and I never saw her
again. Not until Taos at that writer's conference, where after class
we sat eating green chili burgers and fries.

I wondered to her what was it that her father thought the Huichol brought back from the sun. That made her smile.

"What was in the box he carried in his hands?" she repeated.
"What do you think?"

I said, "His heart?"

"Whose heart . . ." she asked, ". . . my father's or the Huichol's?"

"The Huichol's," I answered.

သော ဝေ

Maya and her father, Maurice Livingston III, resided in Santa
Luz. He was a scientist at Los Alamos and a Mayflower descen-
dent. He had married Evelina, an Indian woman from the San Felipe Pueblo whom he had met at the Denver airport. She was an
aspiring poet returning from a reading in Boulder, and he was in
the process of moving to Santa Luz from New Hampshire to start
work on a Defense Department project at Los Alamos.

Evelina and Maurice were sitting next to each other when
they started talking. They hit it off immediately and after that day
spent the next six months seeing each other, frequenting trendy
restaurants, attending art gallery openings and parties of the in-
crowd in Santa Luz.

Theirs was a relationship built on nightly binging, cocaine,
magic mushrooms and all-night fuck marathons. Their hedonism
did not abate, even when Evelina became pregnant and they decided to get married. In fact, the partying got heavier. Maurice's
wealthy parents bought the newlyweds a house close to the Santa
Luz Plaza and were ecstatic at Evelina's pregnancy. She invited
them to the ceremonial dances at San Felipe, to have lunch with

her parents and meet her brothers, all who were Pueblo police-
men. The Livingstons acted like typical tourists and bought
bowls, carpets, turquoise bracelets, rings, necklaces and conch
belts and turquoise bear necklaces from Evelina's cousins.

After the honeymoon, Maurice would drive to Las Alamos in
his new Beamer and lord over the workers. He'd call Evelina at
least four or five times a day to ask about her short stories and a
novel in progress, who she was having lunch with, if the interior
decorator and the landscapers were nearing completion . . . and
sometimes to indulge in a little phone sex—what are you wearing, what color are your panties, open your legs, lay back and
touch yourself, now let me take you from behind, oh, yes, raise
your leg, oh, lick me, suck it . . . etc.

Their cocaine use increased, with Evelina doing almost a
"teener" a day. Despite her addiction, Evelina maintained her reputation among the old white avant-garde and millionaire trust funders around town as an outspoken activist for indigenous people.
They supported her in her political mission and partied with her,
it being fashionable to have an Indian friend, trendier even to have
one so pretty and smart and reckless.

Her poetry readings drew standing-room-only crowds. The
artsy set just could not get enough of her and invited her to gallery
openings, VIP dinners, plays and concerts.

I'd never seen any of this in person. Evelina told me bits and
pieces every time we met to eat or walk on the trails outside Santa
Luz. After Maya was born, Evelina vanished. Nobody knew
where she went, but rumors floated among the people that someone had seen her in Santa Ana Pueblo, Isleta Pueblo, with a cowboy in a truck, in a bar drinking, but no one was certain nor was
there any proof provided that it was really her. She was just gone,
and because of her drug use while pregnant, Maya was born with
certain brain issues far too complicated to tackle in this story. Just
let me say, she had mood swings.

It was about a year after my return that Maya and I met again. We picked up where we had left off years before. Except there was something very wrong with Maya. She was not the wild woman I once knew, the crazy squaw who mounted me and rode me like I was a mustang on the prairie in a lightning storm. She used to be vital, defiant, even disrespectful. But now? She looked down at her papers on the table and her hands and wept, surprising all of us around the table.

"I've changed so much," she said.

Society had tamed her. She'd married a white guy with money and a family name back east. They bought a house in Santa Luz. She was no longer an Indian but an Indian with a white man, an Indian that tourists bought her paintings from, an Indian with a tribal card and an Indian with white man's customs through and through, meaning she loved money and prestige.

ॐ ॐ

When Maya was born she had to stay in the hospital for six months. The infant was premature, undernourished and undersized. She needed round-the-clock care. After they brought the baby home, Evelina became a recluse, did even more drugs, now graduating to the meth pipe and often filling the room with hazardous smoke while her infant daughter slept beside her on the couch.

Maurice lost his patience and divorced her, winning custody of the child. Evelina returned to San Felipe Pueblo, where she started to recover her life, assisted by a shaman. By participating in the shaman's traditional ceremonies, she found her way back to health and to the identity she had before marriage and drugs and baby. She missed her baby girl but had to concentrate on her sobriety. She never spoke a word to her daughter for twenty years.

And as those twenty years went by, Maya married, joined the snobbish elites of Santa Luz, became friends and an advocate for a rich white woman writing Indian novels about Indians. After she discovered her husband having an affair, Maya moved back with her father. It was a temporary separation intended to give her some breathing space.

Meanwhile, Maurice's life at the lab was unchanging, but his home life took a few interesting turns, including becoming obsessed with gardening. There was a well on the property, and he hired a hydrologist to pipe it to serve as irrigation for his garden. One day when the men were working down in the well, Maya climbed down the ladder and was immediately captivated by its charm. The essence of its beauty hung in the air like a heavy presence that was intimate with her. The earth knew her.

Maya's therapists had diagnosed her with an obsessive-compulsive disorder. Whether her fascination with the well was a manifestation of the disorder or not, she would stay longer and longer down in the well, running her fingers along the stones as if she were petting an animal, placing her palms flat against the smooth slabs as if she were trying to speak to them or detect some faraway movement in the stone that would herald the arrival of a cosmic messenger she'd been waiting for.

One day she announced she was moving into the well. Maurice objected adamantly, screaming, threatening, warning her she might end up in a psyche ward.

Maya's obsession did not allow her to sleep or eat until Maurice finally agreed to her descent below ground. He ran an electric line down the well, installed lights, a small refrigerator, folding aluminum chairs and other small portable furniture for her. Actually, Maurice realized he was much more comfortable with her in the well than roaming freely on the streets of Santa Luz. It suited his needs, one in particular.

He loved to gamble but was terrible at it. Despite his mounting losses, he was compelled on payday to visit one of the dozen or so Indian casinos in the area and lose almost his entire paycheck. This led to mind-jarring stress. To lessen his anxiety, Maurice restarted the habits he'd had with Evelina: consuming drugs and escalating to "a little heroin." That is, until a little heroin turned into a lot of heroin and ever-increasing debt to his dealer, who trusted him to pay eventually and enjoyed the accruing interest on the debt from this high-class scientist.

Maurice could not control himself. He was using more, much more, and freaking out, looking out the window at night to see if the police were surrounding his place. Aware that his self-control was limited, he decided to give his stash to Maya to hold until the weekend. He taped up a box of meth and coke, sealed it and gave it to her.

When friends came by to visit and wanted to indulge, he told them he was out, and they countered that they'd gladly pay for it. Eventually, he thought to himself, "How do I sell it to them and not touch it myself until the weekend?" So, he decided to run a string from his house to the well, drop the string down to Maya, and when a client came over to buy, they could pick up their drugs on the well ledge where he would have Maya place it. She'd never know, she'd never see them. She would be innocent, and he'd distance himself from the drugs. It was the perfect plan. He broke up the ounces into twenty-, thirty-, forty- and fifty-dollar papers and a few larger ones, and taught Maya a few secret signals: two tugs meant a twenty-dollar paper, three and four and five would follow accordingly. All Maya had to do was place the drug package on the ledge and never see anyone. It was brilliant.

And it worked, not only to keep him from using his own stash but it also allowed him to pay off his debt. And Maya living below ground with her books, laptop, radio and TV was the best arrangement for the both of them.

Their system was working perfectly. Customers came by and paid, he'd pull the string, she'd place the package on the top ledge, they'd pick it up and drive away. It was such a comfortable and convenient set up that it worked that way for a long time. Maya never came out, she lived down there, talking to the painting of the Huichol dancer she had moved from the house to her well. The Huichol took on flesh and a name and a personality and started to converse with Maya long into the night. Sometimes Maya reached out and touched him, his skin warm, his hands strong and his pulse a kind of radiant ripple.

Then one day climbing up the ladder to deposit a package on the ledge, Maya stopped halfway and turned to her Huichol dancer and said, "I know what you came back with from the sun, and I won't let you do it!" (And what she meant Evelina would never know and could not tell me, when I asked).

Maya sat down on the floor and studied the galvanized pipe outlet the hydrologist had installed a year before, with one pipe running to the tub and toilet and another branching off to the bathroom sink and kitchen faucets. She took her belt, tied her ankle to it and turned on the overflow valve. The water gushed out.

The next morning Maurice walked out of his house and saw water on the walkway flagstones and around his car, flooding the lawn. He followed the trail of flowing water around to the side and behind the house to the well. There it was, water spilling over the ledge, bringing up cosmetic cases and plastic coffee cups, toiletries and clothing articles, letters, journals. There was even a votive candle attached to its cradle dish, the flame flickering as if the whole morning world were its side altar and all of creation the god it prayed to. A white lace dress tangled up around one leg. A hair brush. A toothbrush. He walked closer to the well and saw the naked body of his daughter floating on the surface, a black silk veil sticking to her pale forehead, papers and bits of debris speckling her face, her hands nudging the ledge. There were birds perched on her arms and back pecking at seeds spilled from the spice bottles.

As the water reached her head and pushed it higher, Maya felt a soothing surrender effuse through her heart. She plunged underwater, untied herself, then swam to the ladder. Halfway up she slipped and sank backwards, coming face to face with the Huichol dancer, who smiled at her. He offered her a red tail hawk feather. He opened the box he was carrying and rubbed sunlight on her forehead, a smudge of gold cellular radiance that sparkled and burned through her and filled her being with a warm glow.

She merged into the yellow, a cloud, a white bird. There was a brown pole, its top end red and white and green. She stood on the pole and saw a man in black boots and red, yellow-fringed pants with a green stripe running down the legs. He wore a white shirt and had on a headband of red, green, yellow and blue ribbons that swayed in the wind. His arms were holding a box to his chest, his face inclined downward in reverence to the box's contents. She reached out her arms to take the box.

Sailing away into a sudden lightness, her worries and frustrations and self-doubts floated untethered through space, no longer hers.

"This is how it happens," she thought, "how the remains of my life float away."

Magpie feathers floated by her, then her Tibetan singing bowl with the mala beads she used to finger while sitting cross-legged in meditation. A pack of unopened American Spirits. A black piano key she had found while walking one morning.

The soft weight of water swaddled her and she forgave her mother. The dense indiscretion of water bathed her in a terrifying translucency. She was in the final reckoning and accepted the new order of the jade universe. The ablution swelled with inflammatory and delicious cold in her, and the Huichol opened the box, gesturing with his hand for her to come to Him.

Time passed, and one Spring day I decided to drive out to San Felipe to enjoy the dances on Feast Day. And that's when I saw Evelina. Life hadn't been kind to her; now prematurely wrinkled, she was trying to sell the few remaining teeth she still had with gold fillings to white Indian traders. She was tall, used to have the greatest legs you ever saw on a woman, long, shapely, muscled, best for riding bareback, and when she worked at bartending, those legs of hers in jeans and cowboy boots made customers keep ordering beer just to see her walk on the plank floor toward them. But even her legs were saggy and veined and flabby in those shorts she was wearing. To see her like this was losing a ballet dancer to a car accident.

We sat under a cottonwood and this was the story I relayed to you above, the story Evelina told me, parts of it from what she knew to be true, parts of it from Maya visiting her in her dreams.

"Does she say anything about me when she appears in your dreams?" I asked.

Evelina looked off in the distance to the red mesas. "She wonders how that affair with the girl from the airport worked out."

CLOSE QUARTERS

Drury Plaza Hotel

Mysticism of one sort or another abounds in New Mexico. We've got a mountain of it, but since I've got a pretty good handle on my indigenous way of communing with the spirits, I wasn't expecting to run smack dab into that mountain.

So there I was on I-25, driving to Drury Plaza Hotel in Santa Luz. It was one of those beautiful winter days, and I couldn't have felt any better had I been given Hawaiian dancers and a winning lottery ticket every day. No, this was a perfect setting for my soul to join my ancestors and feel that extreme sensation we call . . . elation? No . . . nirvana? Maybe, but One With God will suffice in my case for this story.

Santa Luz hadn't changed much, and it didn't take me long to find the hotel. A bellman carried in two boxes of my latest books that I planned on giving out for free to the graduates. I hit the front desk; check-in went smoothly. No time for a quick nap—how I wished! Up to my room to freshen up and then to the ballroom for the talk. I walked in, and the kids were everywhere. My eyes traveled over the faces and heads of hundreds of beautiful and brilliant DACA students. They were typical in all ways except one: they represent the very core of what our democracy means.

Most of us are inclined to take our most treasured values for granted. When was the last time you marched for justice? Against police brutality? Environmental justice? Chicanos get beat and jailed every day and most of them are guilty of only one thing: they're poor; they have no money for big-time lawyers (who know how corruption works and can grease its wheels and turn the screws so the wheel of fate turns in their favor—happens every day, we hardly bat an eyelid at it).

I sure felt honored to be asked to speak by people who had fought so hard for the American Dream. So, I gave the best talk of my life, I think . . . if one is to measure it by the fifteen-minute standing applause they gave me, some leaping up and down, whooping as if they were at a rodeo, others whistling and so forth. After giving away a hundred signed books, I took a group picture, shook hands and encouraged them to go and enjoy Santa Luz— after all, their ancestors built this city.

I skipped the banquet, went right up to my room, looking forward to a good night's rest. The second I walked in, I felt movement to my right. I looked at the sofa, the area by the wet bar, the fireplace, and attributed my overly sensitive state to exhaustion. My doctor had warned me to slow down—but whoever listens? If you do, you're not living.

I was washing up in the bathroom, when I heard a baby crying in the adjacent room, the sitting room with a small couch and mini fridge and sink with glasses. I looked around. Nothing. I checked the hallway walk-in closet, turned on the light, decided the cries were coming from next door or down the corridor.

I went back into the bedroom and drew the sheets back, grabbed the remote, hit the sack and before long I was asleep. Soon, I was hearing and seeing weird things in my dreams. I woke up and sat in bed for a bit, wondering what was going on. Then I got up, stepped to the window and looked down at the parking lot. A vague feeling came over me that I'd been there before. There was something familiar about what I was experiencing now. I heard the crying again and this time clearly heard a woman gasping for air. I turned quickly and hurried to the sitting room of my suite. In the dark, I stood in the middle of the room, still as I could be, and listened for more.

I heard it again. "Man, am I tired," I thought, and I went to the bathroom across the hallway from the walk-in closet and filled the tub with hot water. I got in and sank my whole body in until my head was under water. As I surfaced, I heard banging pots and pans in a sink. Then I heard someone slam a coffee cup down when interrupted in the middle of a sentence. He kicked the chair when a woman yelled something, slammed doors and left, yelling, "Stop asking me questions when I'm on the phone!"

I surged out of the water, searched the bathroom, the other room, the bedroom and parking lot. It had to come from the next room or down the hallway, I decided. None of it made sense—all that partying in my younger days was finally catching up.

I dried off, put some boxers on, grabbed a book and read until I was falling asleep, despite hearing the faintest murmurs coming from the sitting room of my suite, as if a ghost was there. Suddenly, a shadow crossed my bedroom doorway entrance. I got up to adjust the thermostat and noticed a heating duct grill on the floor. I heard a pinging and checked the rooms again. On the bathroom counter, decorative glistening pebbles were piled into a pyramid. The mirror was cracked. At different moments, an audible buzzing compressed the space inside and drew out the oxygen. I found it hard to breathe. A woman's voice whispered my name in the darkness. When I turned to locate her face, there was a sucking sound, as if a presence had slipped away, rattling and then flinging open the windowpanes overlooking the parking lot.

I moved to the window—Who had opened it?—and that's when I saw my grandpa walking across what was no longer the lot I had parked in but now an open field with a few sheep grazing in it. He was walking in the dark through the fields on his way to work. At the far end, where the Arts Academy of Santa

Luz should have been, stood the old, red-bricked two-story school where my grandpa worked his second job as janitor. He cleaned the classrooms, emptied trash cans and dust-mopped the halls. He had always dreamed that I'd learn to read and write, yet I don't think he ever envisioned that I'd have dozens of books of poems and be accepted as an intellectual speaking to groups of students and literary types. I imagined his calloused hands applauding and saying, *"Eso sí, m'ijito, ese es mi hijo."* That's right, that's my boy.

It was dark in my hotel room. When I locked the window and closed the curtains, I heard someone sobbing in the other room on the couch. When I went to inspect it, I found a woman sitting on the floor, legs spread apart with blood all over her nightgown around her vagina. Wedding photos and letters were scattered around her on the floor. The air was thick with cigarette smoke. There was a glass of Seagram's next to an ashtray stuffed with Pall Mall cigarette butts. She did not look up, just stared at the papers.

I was totally freaked out and I knelt by my bedside and closed my eyes and prayed for the Lord to intervene and bring back my sanity. This is what it felt like when a person goes crazy, and right before my eyes my whole life was collapsing around me. I expected that in short time I'd be strapped to a gurney and headed for Las Vegas, the state mental hospital.

"The hallucinations have to stop," I told myself. I didn't know what to do. I got back in bed and stared into the dark, hoping the room would stop spinning, the floor would stop shaking. I felt the footsteps in the ante room stop pacing. My dizziness passed. I gazed to my right at the glistening frost on the window and noticed how the moonlight refracted in a million shards and thorns. Then I remembered: days and nights in close quarters, and everywhere on the floor, the table, the dirt outside, the sink counter and stove, the tub, clammy and sticky sheets and pillow cases tousled . . . my parents' clothes strewn all around the house, her flesh constantly touching his, hair and juices and bones and teeth and tongues in his and over hers, cigarette smoke and gin and wine and the cool night air; the dense, earthy smell, claustrophobic humidity, the howl of barking dogs in the foothills, a quick and violent flapping of owl wings. . . . I felt all of this around me in that hotel room, merging with it.

It was the first time hearing my mother. I could not explain any of it—as if this room was a cave and the roar inside was her voice, way at the back in the darkness, the sole sane element in my otherwise crazy life. As a child, it had grounded me when she rocked me back and forth in her arms, affirming my belief that there was hope beyond the Santa Luz streets, beyond the prairie that surrounded us, beyond the windmills and forest. There was the possibility of another existence out there, and it struck me with such clarity and space and truth: my hotel used to be St. Vincent Hospital, and this was the room where I was born.

THE INTERVIEW

Wish you could choose your neighbors, but you can't unless you're rich enough to buy a thousand-acre ranch in Oregon, where you can step out, do your yoga looking at the ocean—or in urban parlance, lock yourself up in a gated community, water your grass each morning in your housecoat and jammies, wave to those other cut-outs watering their grass in their jammies . . . Cancel that for a poor writer—you're lucky if you have a cup-size windowsill cactus. You have no book, scant income, you're a closet poet, you move where you can get in with a reasonable deposit and without a credit check. Otherwise, it's the streets for you, buddy, or, in a makeshift lean-to made of mesquite and pinon branches, a walking skeleton in a loin cloth wandering about babbling about end of times. Barring that, you can't predict who's going to come knocking on your door with a plate of fresh cooked marijuana cookies, like my neighbor Sandra did.

She was my neighbor, fat and short with long hair and a nose that could cause real damage if it bumped into you. I'm serious: it was a war zone nose that could be mistaken for a nuclear warhead. Regardless, I adapted to her intrusions each day when she banged on the screen door for our evening walks; as she would say, "A little exercise to digest our food." I could understand seeing her duck-step, not because it was a pattern drawn from a life of walking that way since childhood, but because her weight called for a step . . . step . . . step cadence in order to keep the load moving. (One look at this beer belly of mine, even though I

67

hardly touch beer, and you'll know that I know what I'm talking about.)

I anticipated everything on our very first walk, except her unending unruliness and aggressive opinions on every topic from tacos to Trump.

She started in. "I'm a bitter old bitch, and it's not something I apologize for. If you had to deal with the shit I have to, you'd know, you'd know . . .

"Take for instance this airport bullshit. I'm a driver, I pick people up at the airport and drive them to their destination. I don't have to turn Fox news on to hear a bunch of old white guys screaming hatred at everyone not white: I get it.

"If I'm not driving some prick that his daddy gave too much to, or some asshole who fucked us all, working on Wall Street or at a bank. I'm on the internet working for a debt collections agency—I love it. It's like therapy for me, getting these losers who think they can walk off without paying their debts.

"One of them happened to be a neighbor, who I rarely see, since I'm driving some bitch from the airport to Santa Luz or Los Alamos. But there he was, this better-than-thou cocksucker who owed my parents money. My parents are old and need to die, they creep along, falling in the bathroom and moaning for hours until someone hears them. . . . They scratch themselves and bleed out because of their blood thinner meds. . . . But there is no reason not to pay them. You should. And why? Not because of high moral standing or anything like that. The quicker you pay them, the faster I can hire someone to care for them.

"Do you realize how hard it is to walk them, toddling along, an inch at a time, and act like I care? Die already. We give way too much credit to the importance of our parents' longevity. Look, they've lived, they drank and fucked and shopped. . . . So, die already, be done with the Florida disease of wanting to live forever, and with this Hollywood epidemic of facelifts and trying to look thirty when you're eighty and shitting and pissing your pants. I mean, what the fuck's wrong with us, right?

"You can see me carefully holding my mother's arm by her elbow as I walk her around the block. You can catch me dressing my father, handing him his pills, making sure he takes them all. But, really, what are my thoughts?

"I shouldn't say. My girlfriend nags me. I nag her. She says I'm a lesbo frickin' bitch, and if you define a bitch by having a pussy, then I'm one. She's my bitch, the two of us live together.

"And you'd think these jerks, these financial twats, these high-dollar businessmen stealing our money would know a lesbian when they see one? No, they hint they're open to night company and would buy me dinner—its scaredy-cat talk for 'wanna fuck,' when I'm driving them to their hotel in Santa Luz, or a casino, or to some conference where they can all caress their tiny dicks and imagine fucking a woman or getting fucked by another man.

"If they only knew. I'd pull over and fuck them under a railroad trestle and make them my bitches. If they only knew I could fuck the teeth right out of them—yes, I could. My girl always tells me how mean I am, that even my iPhone wouldn't want me if it had a choice. Even my panties, if they had a choice. I fucked her so hard I dislocated her shoulder one night.

"But who cares what people or machines think. I hold a sign up at the bottom of the escalator at the airport as I wait for some company man to descend and smile at me and say, 'That's me.' I grab his bags. I open the limo door. I tune the radio to his music. I offer him a bottle of water, thinking the whole time, I mean, while being so nice and ingratiating and exhilarating to him with my good manners, that I think he's beneath the shit I take each night after eating crappy fast food from a machine at the hospital cafeteria, where I sometimes eat when taking my parents for their check-ups.

"You'd think after all these years of driving important people and calling losers to pay their debts, I'd be happy? Well, let's just go down the line and tell you why I'm not. 'Die already,' is my life motto. Skip sentimentality and bury your ass. I mean, you're wasting money that I could be using, you know. You've had yours, now give me mine. I'm your daughter, jeez, give it a break, enough weeping in your teacup or whisky glass. I've earned it taking care of you.

"But going back to that damn driving job of mine, here's a few tips for ignoramuses wanting to follow in my esteemed career: never allow your true self-expression to come out. You gotta develop a higher sense of lying, sort of a false presentation; otherwise, you'll never make it. Unless you're a politician, then it's a natural fit. You gotta be grandiose. Tell your passenger, 'Sure, sure, been there, done that, lost millions, used to own a casino back when, married and divorced, she took it all,' that sort of thing.

"Takes time to learn how to hide your rage at the world. And your aggression? Got no problem there. I take it out on my girl-friend. I mean who wouldn't get mad with one's whole life a disappointment, right? Driving and debt collecting. . . . Had I known at birth this was my fate, I would have dropped myself from a building roof or stabbed myself with the knife they used to cut my umbilical cord. I get passengers with so much grandiosity and superiority, I sometimes drive all the way to their hotel smiling at the fantasies I conjure on ways to torture them. I keep hearing this phrase from them: They're 'entitled' . . . either to better treatment from the kids or wife or boss. Their world revolves around what they're entitled to.

"I mean, don't you get sick of that? Really, be honest. You do, right? Just can't stomach hearing how so and so shamed them. And, oh, those Los Alamos ones, they speak so timidly and talk about their vulnerability. . . . They outta be in Seinfield's comedy or on some therapy show or maybe even Oprah, how their compassion is abused, and their kid really set them back, cost a fortune to fuel his failures.

"I wish it was legal to run over people. See someone you'd like—maybe the coat they're wearing, the way they trim their beard, hold their wife's hand at the corner waiting for the light to change—run 'em over, best on Christmas Eve.

"I know what you're thinking. Who let this person talk? I didn't ask, remember, you walk with me and we talk and this is what my life looks like—smells like, really. Dead, huh? You wanted me to talk about things, so I am. I'm a Trump voter. They were trying to find someone who liked Trump, and they found me. This guy is writing a book of interviews or something and he wanted to pay people to talk about why they like Trump. I met him on the phone, trying to pay off on a debt. His last book was on successful people, and I saw it, had his picture on the back flap. So who's going to turn down a little pocket change, right?

"So Trump, yeah. Here's what I told him. I like him because I like someone, if he doesn't get his way, he gets pissed and starts raping and beating people up. I think it's a good example for kids who wanna get ahead. You know, you don't get your way? Then get fucking mad. How else you gonna get ahead in this world? And don't take shit. The second someone drops a dime on you, wring that fucker's neck. Absolutely no disagreements tolerated—you're right and that's that. Too many chiefs, and you don't get anything done. One boss, that's me. No back talk. You see someone else here? No. So, talk to me, I'm here, I'm the center of this business, nothing happens unless I say so. That's the attitude. No consensus crap or building agreement bullshit. I'm the go-to momma. And don't think for a minute I can't make my own rules. I can violate any boundary you set up. Otherwise, how can we progress? It's a process, my friend. I break the rules to make new ones. That's why I like Trump: he don't care, he just goes out and breaks any rule he wants to and doesn't look back. Love him. There is no such thing as a boundary he likes: the more he breaks,

the more I realize he's responsible for making things right. And
sometimes making things right means you gotta take actions
other people are too coward to take. I mean, I love Trump for the
way he takes control of shit. Don't you? He just goes in there and
says this is mine . . . like his taxes, never showed them, and all
those things he says. . . . Who cares if they're made up. They
might be real, who are we to say? Since when do we know what
is really going on up there in that White House? I think we're
sticking our nose where it don't belong. Let him do what he's got
to do. He's unique, you know, a special kind of man. All the ladies
dream about that man . . . touching and holding him, you know?
Them saying stuff about him, that's just bitterness at not being
able to have him, you know? I know, happens to me sometimes,
some chick wants me, sees me dressed in my driver's cap and
black coat and looks me all up and down and sweet, them watery
eyes telling me, 'Take me, momma.' Sort of like I'm above the
others in the world—that's how he must feel I bet, Trump. I bet
we'd get along good.

"That's why I agreed to do this survey. Maybe, you never
know, he'll read it and call me . . . you never know. I mean, he's
like family, we think the same. We know how to use our God-
given talents, use others too, for good, you know? And, sure, people are going to say bad things, but only 'cause they're not grown,
don't understand that when it's time, you gotta go. Called matu-
rity. When it's time, it's time. I'm not exploiting you or betraying
you. I just don't see any sense in wasting time when there's nothing there anymore. Sure, we might have had something (like them
European treaties and allied agreements with the UN or nukes
and stuff), but like the saying goes, 'The thrill is gone.' It's gone
and it's time to move on, no looking back. That's being a grown
up. Cut your losses and move on. I'm what they call a higher
functioning human being. If you don't get what I'm saying the
first time, you ain't never gonna get it. I'll take your loneliness

away, but you can't make a career outta loving me. I don't wanna miss an opportunity by hanging around you. Once we're done, I go. That's what he's telling China . . . Mexico . . . See what I'm saying? This ain't no rejection, this is true to point in fact that I'm important and gotta get the passenger to the next stop and the loser to pay his bills . . . and momma and daddy to die already.

SUNDAYS AT GERALD'S HOUSE

I joined a group of writers and poets in Santa Luz and we'd meet every Sunday to hang out and talk writing. We'd go over to Gerald's house for dinner. We'd all bring a dish. Mine was always green chili stew, which he loved and couldn't get enough of.

He was a nut, and I say this in reverence and awe for the man himself and his work. Not many really knew him. Although, when he was young, he gave hundreds of interviews, and his books were published in more than 28 languages. I'd say not one of his readers or publishers knew the man. He was an oddity, a newborn star every morning he got out of bed.

As soon as we ate, without clearing the dishes or anything, we were all dying to hear his opinions on our work. Most of us at the table dreamed of being published. Most of us wanted, more than anything in the world, to finish the work we were doing. Most of us happened to be enslaved to it for years before being invited to sit at Gerald's table. He loved telling us, "I invite only those who are not writers, I would never have a writer sit at my table."

By this I think he meant we had to come to his table with a life that said something, with experiences where we were tested and proven to be cowards in some instants, and in others, as brave a warrior as the Aztecs ever boasted.

After making his green tea—he loved his green tea!—Gerald would begin, leaning his elbows on the table, and with a serious and impassioned face, he'd start with the writer whose turn it was—we rotated weekly.

"Now, Joe, I'm going to give you something really, really hard to do: an assignment. It's going to be really hard to do, but I think you can do it." He'd pause to get a reaction from Joe.

"Okay," Joe would say.

"In Part One, the very first sentence of your novel is, 'The world begins with music.' Now, what I want you to do with that one sentence, I want you to use your imagination and I want you to go to your mother's womb, before you even existed, and I want you to write me something about the night you imagine you were conceived. And I want you to write that, too, all those little things that go into a woman, and if one of them breaks through that wall, then you are conceived."

"Yeah," Joe says.

"Then you are inside your mother's body, and all the sounds that happen in that environment. The blood pulsing, the heart, the stomach . . . when you were conceived. I want to see if you can write that scene musically. If the world in fact begins with music, then write that scene after that sentence. I don't know if you hear music outside of your mother's body. I don't know if you can write that scene. It will be an amazing achievement if you can write that scene."

"It was an allegorical sentence. I didn't mean it literally. I don't really want to do that, to be honest," Joe countered.

"I know you don't want to do it. I read . . ."

"I mean, you know the Bible says the world began with God and the world was God, but it doesn't go on to describe God and the universe and what it sounded like?"

"Wouldn't that be great, though? Wouldn't it be great?"

"No, because the whole chapter is music!"

"I thought I would ask you to do that, create a night or a day where you were conceived and were completely surrounded with sound."

"I have a part that I think you read where I talk about my memory of hearing angels singing, or maybe my mother singing to me. I think that's more what I mean."

"Yeah, I have that."

"I mean, I'd be willing to stand by the fact the world begins with music, but only in the broadest sense."

"All right. I just thought it would be a hell of an achievement to pull that baby off. Let's go to 'Beautiful Enemies' then. So I can focus, read the first paragraph."

"I'm seated in the armchair at the foot of my mom's bed, a cheap nylon string guitar on my knee, playing a song I just learned. Maybe 'Fire and Rain' or 'Sound of Silence.' Mom's eyes shined like river stones as I strummed cords and warbled the melodies with my husky mediocre voice. There is a cold current washing our way. Songs are a bridge across that wide water."

"I want you to tell me how old you are seated in the armchair at the foot of the bed. Since I know the background to this story somewhat, I want to hear more about those cheap nylon strings and the guitar on your knee. Your mom is in bed sick, right? You're holding the guitar, right?"

"Yeah."

"I'm just thinking that the guitar is the only thing holding you to the earth. As the reader, I want to feel that. Go to the end of the second paragraph. I've got that marked. I've got the feel of the cedar of the guitar's back resonating against my solar plexus."

"Yeah."

"The line, '. . . words cast a melody, the way the harmony puts pain into the words blue, or green, or grey. The way you have to synchronize your two hands to create a groove, and how that groove seems to interject life into the room.' When you structure a story, you have to move stuff around sometimes, and if something fits better somewhere else, you know, part of structuring, the editing part, is one of the most difficult things in the world."

"Right."

"I want to see the room a lot better. I want to *see* that room. I want that room to be a vignette in my mind that almost becomes archetypal. I want to see a kid in that room and I want to see the

room in a way I've never seen a room in my life. You've hit the
time of day with the light, you hit the fact that your mom is in
bed. But, you know what? You go into a lot of other stuff. You
move the story along, but I don't think you should be moving it at
that point. I think you have to stay in that damn room. I want you
to tell me what your mom's toenails look like, the calluses on her
feet, her hands. I want to know what the pictures look like. I want
to know what the door looks like. Does it have the old-fashioned
black doorknob with the skeleton key? I want to know what's
hanging in that room. I want to know what happened in that room.
I want to know that room! I want to know her in that room with
you. The only thing that saves you two from each other, from that
time in that room, the only thing that saves you from the horrible
consciousness that is a frozen moment in time . . . is music. She's
going one way and you are going another, and the only way to
keep the connection is through the music, somehow, someway. I
want to know the vulnerabilities of that kid and how that guitar
and that music ground him, so he doesn't go absolutely crazy in
that room. I mean, you write about it, but you write about it as if
it's a pretty easy thing to handle.

"I don't know about you, but it would be a really tough thing for
me to handle. I would write from the struggle of this kid. He's got
to create some sort of defense system, and it is always the music.

"Does that room have secrets? Is it a box, a container that carries the secrets that won't spill out to anybody, and does the little
boy know that? He says here, 'My sister and brother and I are tip-
toeing around as if a loud sound will crack the house. She has
spells, and when she needs to rest, something that's been living inside her seems to escape. I can sense much that I can't name.'

"You don't want to say that. Tell me what you sense in that
room. That's the writer's job. I want you to sense what's going on
in that room and just blow the reader's mind. So many of us sense
something in a room, but nobody has ever taken the time to write
it. You know?

"I'm seated in the armchair at the foot of my mother's bed, and what I would do is write about the bed in a way that is unforgettable. I would write about the blankets that cover her in a way that's unforgettable. I would stay with the bed, you know? Then I would use a transition to somehow show the only thing keeping you from falling out of your chair: the guitar. Then, I'd go to the guitar. Was the bed wooden? How is the guitar connected to it? There has to be connectives here.

"Then Jimmy Hendrix dies. That marks time. Then you go back to here, he's lying on top of a white quilt, 'autumn's afternoon light streaming through the tall trees and into the windows, the church steeple' . . . That is really great, but it just seems to leave me too soon. The churches' steeple visible from her bedroom . . . If my mom was lying in bed, I would think about that damn church and her going to heaven. I would think about, right then and there, why the hell did God make her suffer so much? There's the steeple right there. If the steeple is made out of the same damn wood that my guitar is, I can do better than God. I can at least sing to her. What have you done, except take her money every Sunday? Do you understand?"

"Right."

"It's those connections."

"I agree with all that, but it's a three-hundred-page book. A lot of the stuff that you're talking about I'm going to get to. It's the building up of that."

"That's okay, if you want to take that door out, you can take that door out. All I'm telling you, if you want to exit through that door, you can. All I'm saying is, I would have a hard time moving on if I was writing this scene."

"I guess I'm worried about front loading the story with all that detail. Maybe I just want to move on too fast."

"If you're going to open the book with you in front of your mom, it must be with formidable archetypes. You recognize that she's finite, she's not going to be here. Don't worry about the length or what the reader is going to think. You need to satisfy your own sense of storytelling. I'm pointing out certain things that I think could lead. It's sort of a fulcrum, an epicenter."

"The archetype from which the whole story would emerge? Spend more time building the foundation with a certain intimacy and detail?"

"Absolutely. I think that room carries all the themes of the book. At the end of the story, that little boy is still going to be playing music to raise her from the dead. That little boy, I honestly believe in my heart, thinks that there is a chance that music could cure her, in that room, right there."

"Yeah, I think it's well worth doing, the more you talk . . . I'm understanding what you're seeing."

"Well, here's the problem, Joe. I'm playing devil's advocate because I'm trying to get you to write at the highest level you can write. More importantly, I'm trying to get you to write at the highest level you *want* to write at. There comes a point in time when you don't want to go there anymore. You are dealing with a fanatic on this end. If there is a beautiful scene, I want to push it and push it to where it breaks apart into fragments. You can't take who I am and what I'm saying and adopt it into your consciousness. You have to come to terms with yourself on how you want to tell the story. That is what I admire the most. I want something I know was carefully crafted. Let's go on. 'There's a cold current washing our way,' 'songs are a bridge across that white water.'

"That's beautiful, man, that's beautiful. The next sentence says she's lying on top of a white quilt. You know, the year with Jimi Hendrix works well—I like that. But that last word died, it really does beg for the little guy looking up at his mom's face and wondering if she's going to meet Jimi Hendrix. Is she going to listen to him? There has got to be a connection here. You know, is she going to get to see him play? If that makes him happy . . . like, 'Mom, get me an autograph, hold on to it for me,' you know? 'Tell him how much I love him.' Something like that brings something else into this. Cut across stuff, you know? You are looking for an intersection. I'm just saying. The steeple, you see what I'm saying about that steeple? The way they package death, if you can pay for it, you're going to have a good death."

"Yeah."

"And as a novelist, as a memoirist, you should be able to nail that when you look at it."

"The really hard part is that at that age, I did not have that awareness. Back then, I was still naïve and young, and so if I'm really describing how I saw that in that moment, it's going to be different from how I see it now."

"That's perfect! Why don't you write that he doesn't know? You were looking at a steeple and the only thing that came into your mind or heart I suppose was 'God, have mercy on your mother.' Prayers float down to her in some way."

"Oh, I can, I guess, but who's speaking in the scene? I think the truth is, the overseeing eye and the thirteen-year-old speak together."

"There is a way of transcending time and space as a narrator. As a narrator, you can use time and space any way you want."

"Right."

"You can keep the kid in that room. But even if you do keep the kid in that room, you're still falling short of telling the reader what the kid is really experiencing emotionally."

"Right."

"Every single young adult book about a kid is written by an adult. How do you explain that contradiction? How do you go there? Write about the kid in a way that brings a lot of experience bearing down on it. If you want to hurry through the scene, that's great, get to a scene that's pivotal to the book. If you're going to open up with this scene, which I think is a fabulous place to open up, I would bear down on it."

"I see what you're saying. I don't always know when to stay with a scene. I do know that the deeper I get into a scene, the more that I feel that my own writer's heart is speaking, and I think that's something that you're encouraging. In your own book, you tear open a lot of these vulnerable spaces. I feel that maybe one of the reasons I hurry through it is that I don't want to remember that. It is an unconscious fear. One of the beautiful things about writing for a kid that age is that they see the problem. The problem is called a literary existential enigma. This is the problem *I'm* having."

"There are a few things that will be thematic narrative spines for the book. One of them is the guitar."

"Yeah, absolutely!"

"That's it there! You go, brother! The other thing you want going all the way through is the bridge."

"Right."

"Sometimes that bridge is going to be burned down. Sometimes you yourself are going to take out your bowie knife and cut it. I don't know who's going to be standing on the bridge when you cut it. Sometimes that bridge is going to go, and there's going to be people on it and they're going to fall."

"Right."

"Other times that bridge is going to be weak and the ropes are going to be frail. Some people are going to have to dare themselves to go across it because they want to be with you. They want to be part of your life. They are taking a big chance by going to you, because you're this crazy dude trying to find his way through the world with a guitar, and that's no easy chore to do. The people that cross the bridge, they see the bridge, they love the bridge, but they don't know if it will tear loose. That's a thematic narrative spine for the book. That's one of them. We'll talk about where you go with that.

"The other one is your mom. Your father is a shadow. I want you to write about your father in an almost opposite sort of discordance. In a way that he is not there, all you ever see are remnants of him. The belt, the cigarette butts, the ashtray, a coffee cup, but you never see the man. You see the empty shoes; you see the sadness in your moms' eyes. You only see the remnants of the man; you never see the man. So, don't use the shadow of the father, use these remnants of him. He is supposed to be your father but he is never seen. But he's never seen."

"Yeah."

"Do you live by your senses? Do you make your decisions based on what you sense or feel?"

"Yes, yes."

"Then you've got to bring the senses out and write about them instead of downplaying them. That should be a thematic aspect of the narrative spine. You sense so much that you can't put into words but you can dig deeper."

"Right."

"The senses are a big deal in your book. I'm the opposite as a writer. I don't sense anything; I draw it out. If I think there is a spirit in the room, I'll talk to it. That's why I've had nine wives; they walk in and hear me talking to a beautiful girl and then they file for divorce."

(Everyone laughs).

"The whole way I planned it before," Joe said, "I think I know why you're challenging that. I was sneaking in the whole idea of my mother's death. The main character is twenty years old. There is an enormous denial going on, as many of us do, using music as both an escape and a way to dig deep. What you're saying is to get a bit deeper into it, to be plunged into the beating heart of this scene and have all the blood of this scene spread out like rivulets of a river through the whole book. Start intense."

"I agree. I don't think you ought to sneak it in. I don't know why, as writers, what we hold most precious we bring in little by little. I don't like that. Let's just put it on the table.

"Denial is what makes up a great memoir. If we can close that book at the end of the night and are like . . . you have to read this . . . you are nailing our emotions, our fragilities or vulnerabilities, and our fears. . . . We are afraid of our parents dying, we're afraid to take care of them. I don't know how we got afraid, but we are. What you are going to be writing about is a guy who had a really hard time coming to terms with taking care of his ailing mother. That was just one thematic strength of this book.

"This guy, this musician, tried every way he could to run away from it, but in the morning, it was there every time he looked out the window. He saw her in that bed again. That is where the music came from. His inability to cope with his mother leaving, his inability to deal with it is when the guitar becomes important. That's another theme. It's a young man taking care of his mother."

"Right."

"That's beautiful. I sure love books. Memoirs where the woman, the daughter, becomes the best friend of her mother during that period are beautiful. I've also read other books where the bell tolls, and the guy has to come in from Wall Street to see his father. He's a badass wolf on Wall Street, but he is a kid buried in that. I want this to happen in your book. I want to see this kid get that climax moment in the middle of the book. He breaks down and says what he didn't get. You know? What he didn't get or give. Maybe that is your music, maybe it is a redemption."

⁌ ⁌

On the drive home, I couldn't get that little boy of out of my mind, that steeple, the guitar, the room. I was a little scared, because next week was my turn, and it's easy to sit and listen, but when Gerald starts in on my work, it'll be like dancing on fire. I might get burned, but it sure would make living interesting and life full of mystery and writing the greatest passion of all things in life.

SANTA LUZ HUSTLES &
LA MEMORIES

"It's reflected in No. 45 in the Oval Office. That's why we've got so many more kids picking up guns: they see him, a creature with no scruples, no ethics, destroying everything it touches."

That was pretty much the discussion we had at Orley's place last night, and on my walk to the bus station I knew it was time to leave LA. Like so many other screenwriters, I too had arrived here with dreams of making a score. One movie with my name on the screen as screenwriter and I could have enough money to do what I really came to LA to do: write the novel about my pops, who I never got along with. Or rather, he really didn't like me. Or it seemed so because he never hung out with me, no baseball at parks, no swing set in the backyard, no sitting around watching a movie, no talk, nothing. Crazy as it sounds, he was a stranger even after my living with him all those years. So, I wanted to explore that, and that was why I made the move, went to LA. But I ended up being the same loser as all the other losers in this town, wanting to do something my heart commanded and ignoring those commands daily because I never had enough courage.

The reason I hadn't started the novel, I rationalized, was I hadn't gotten a contract to write a movie. It was a head game I enjoyed playing with myself, seeing myself fail every day and saying not to worry, telling myself this was how the game was played: keep submitting my screenplay. . . . I was the guy you

85

see smiling in all those photos, all of us in some way connected to the movie industry. I was the guy who went to bed with a different chick every night—they were everywhere: recent arrivals, old lionesses getting beat down every day by a director or producer and tolerating the abuse because they dreamed one day of having some kind of shot as a showrunner, or maybe, after years of getting shouted at and bawled out, curses raining down on their graying heads, they held on because they believed that they could nail down a job one day at the directors guild or writers guild. But only if, *only if* they put up with all the shit. Others had, why not them?

And so, we all held on, the gays trying to be writers really getting into their gay strutting, writing for the *LA Times* and disparaging non-gays (as if non-gays had no clue about fashion, food, culture, movies and books), promoting the LGBTQ movement over all else, as if no gays had ever lived before, as if being gay was like discovering a new planet with human life on it. . . . And now, we were all saved, we were all redeemed by the gays because they were so intelligent, so cultured, so understanding and forgiving and sensitive.

And I was okay with that, since I knew the feeling of being overlooked and also of looking over everyone else, being powerful and powerless. I had experienced them both and felt happy for the gays now that they were in the main street parade. It was cool. It gave a little life to an otherwise decrepit and aging Hollywood society, where all everyone talked about was their latest hair-plant or facelift and who to recommend for a divorce lawyer.

I couldn't wait to leave. My last night in LA, I sat in the Blue Room bar sipping a margarita and remembering the night I took a red-haired, blue-eyed Irish woman out to the parking lot. We fucked in my car. Her father had invented the Steadicam or some such thing. She was a make-up artist. Little did I know then that she would follow me out to Santa Luz months after I arrived. There were so many women who came out to Hollywood and

fucked as habitually as eating a bagel. That's the kind of people
we were: we didn't notice things, we didn't have real lives, we
had ambitions, we wanted to write books and be millionaires and
invest in start-ups, partner up with other rich guys and overlook
the bay in Seattle. For our bi-annual meeting we'd act like there
were no wars in the world, no racism, no homelessness, no climate change. The money was too good, too real, and it burned
any memory out of us that might have been present before we
became wealthy.

In the bar now reminiscing, I looked around at the others having drinks, the most god-awful glum hopelessness in their eyes.
I could see they too were only trying to hang on until something
broke, something gave, some hoary God decided it was time to
give them an opportunity to prove themselves as real writers, actors, directors, etc.

I couldn't wait, though, so I moved to Santa Luz, New Mexico. A lot of my acquaintances were moving here because it was
fashionable, not because they were from here like I was.

Coming over the La Jornada del Muerto, the city of Santa
Luz in the distance below said to me, yes, welcome back, your return was not as you had wished (successful), but you are back, my
son. Here in the place where you were baptized. You had forgotten that this city was once yours, filled with brown people, now
occupied by whites who have taken it all, with their money and
power and racist attitudes. Have you come back to reclaim your
roots? Much like a violin player, alone on the night streets, obsessed by the sadness of the world and all its sorrows, you play
and turn and twirl and the inhabitants of this city all stand at their
doors and windows and look on you with the nostalgic despair
that they once felt, what you play in every violin note. . . . They
once believed, they once breathed, and they once pursued each
trembling note you fling like red-hot blazing heartseeds off your
strings. . . . Once, once, once; it seems all life can be defined by
once.

As you drove down that long hill into Santa Luz, the city said, "How you enjoyed me once, how you loved as a boy to sit next to a nopal cactus or sage bush in the desert and smell the wind and smell the pinons. The fragrance they emitted was so overwhelming, it made you cry out sometimes and run full speed for no reason other than that you were so happy. You couldn't contain the joy in your tiny legs. The wind, the dirt, the scrub brush, the stones, the hawks and the small birds made you weep tears so pure, pure as water was when it first was created. Standing in the chill dawn and staring at the sun rise on the horizon, your cheeks chilled stiff and your skin rough as a rock; heavy-lipped, stiff-lidded, you cried looking at your land, like a small emperor, an Aztec lord, Inca royalty, a Mayan priestess. . . .

Purpose tears. Raza tears. Earth-belonging boy tears. Brown parent tears, indigenous tears made of dance steps, made of gourd rattles, tears made of piano keys and Ludovico playing on the same canyon boulder echoing all the way out to the universe, striking God's ears and making him smile . . . those tears were once yours.

And now? No more thinking about injustice or racism or white vigilantes, it was all about paying rent and staking out my piece of the pie, getting what money I could to take care of my shit. Coming down the long hill into Santa Luz, I could hear my LA buddies' voices in my head talk about how many movies were being made here, how many directors lived here, actors too, and at any given time there might be dozens of movies filmed here.

So, I had as good a chance as anyone at making it here. When I googled it, I found out there were something like sixty-eight movies being shot here—true, most of them were grimy, slop sink hubris, but hey, who really gives a shit anymore about movies, good *or* bad? They fill time up, they allow us to forget our own little lives, stewed like carrots in this big pot of *caldo* where everyone gets a daily bowl. Who am I to be picky? You know what I mean?

There's a time and place for that, and I definitely don't qualify for either—no reason really, I just don't. I got real with myself: the industry can't handle wild boys like me. It needs
kneelers, the ones who will kneel down and do whatever it takes
to grab a job—kneel down and . . . you fill in the blank.

I came back determined to become a kneeler. To be a copious
bowing *sí, señor* servant to the powerful and make them believe
I really think they're smarter than me, make them believe they
have special attributes that exceed my human flaws, make them
believe that I'm inferior and fated and born to serve them and fulfill their wishes. And at the end of the week, I'd cash my check,
baby. I'd get what I needed at the end of the day. So what if I
didn't have any pride, self-respect, dignity? So what if I'd deplete
my reserves of what little integrity I still had? So what? It's called
life, baby, and getting real.

Within a few days I rented myself a nice little southwestern
pink adobe. I joined a bunch of other losers, and we all crowded
together in a community meeting each evening to suck wine and
tell lies about how we were almost there, how so-and-so was really interested in our screenplay. Then we'd return to our little
rooms at night to stand before our mirrors, trying on clothes we'd
bought at second-hand stores in the plaza. We'd model ourselves
in the glass as Frida Kahlo, John Wayne, a cool hippie with beads
and turquoise, a rich, ugly woman in a mid-life crisis. We'd try on
our fancy boots, designer jeans, gem-studded vests and cowboy
hats, speaking aloud to the mirror, to an imagined boy at the bar,
asking how much he required for a quick fuck. . . .

I thought during those bleak days that I'd seen it all and often
thought, that's it, I'm throwing the towel in. But then I met this
professor at a party. He was smoking meth from a glass bowl,
while his wife was splashing paint on a canvas pretending to be
O'Keefe; wiry jaws, sunken eye-sockets, huge lips that had been
filled with something to make them look like balloons. He of-

fered me a part-time gig at the American Indian College teaching screenwriting.

Hell yeah I smoked the meth, let his wife suck me (she wore white gloves!). . . .

Ahh, we're here in this city where the conquistadores came and subdued the Indians. This city where the Indians sell jewelry and hawk their wares on the plaza. This city where it seems like every Wolf of Wall Street has come to live. This city where the rich all live on the east side and the poor and indigenous are shoved off to the west side or way out to the margins because they can't afford the rents anymore. Philanthropists, trust-fund grown men who want Mommy's nipple every day, the emaciated crystal chanters, horny yoga contortionist orgasming at the instructor's touch, refugees and immigrants, chili lovers and art collectors, powerful and rich white drug dealers, tribal council members as corrupt as any inquisitor, Indian sculptors going from bar to bar offering their buffalo and eagle dancer pieces to tourists to make enough money to buy their drugs, marijuana growers . . .

Come to me, my sweet little woman, let us all gather in one big chummy family each night at million-dollar homes to drink and fuck and lie and try to forget our lives, to bury ourselves under drugs and kneel down too many times and look in the mirror and see ourselves getting older and more helpless and desperate and thinking, if we take more drugs, spend more money at the pharmacy and at the plastic surgeon, it will all change.

My first week teaching I met Norman, a guy about my age (31) who blew me away and changed my life forever. He told me that he was the first of his people to walk the surface of the Earth. He came from the bottom of the Grand Canyon and was the first of his family to climb up and walk on the ground above; all the rest had never climbed up there. They had lived down below the old way, growing their corn and drinking fresh water from the river as far back as memory could recall.

I asked Norman if he would be willing to collaborate with me on a screenplay. He agreed, and that meant we had to get an agent, one of those loathsome creatures who crawl out each night from their webs to snatch butterflies and eat their wings. Nevertheless, I set out to do whatever it would take. I was determined to give it one more earnest shot. I hoped I had enough balls and integrity left to start my life over with a little "get-realness." I started by asking around to see if anyone could recommend an agent.

One night I found myself rolling a joint at the table of a publisher who was into mountain climbing. He had spent a fortune flying around the world to climb to the highest summits. He was the ugliest son-of-a-bitch I'd ever met. But he was a friend, and that excused all character and physical faults. And here I was at his table, drinking cheap wine and listening to his stories. When I asked him about film agents, he said he didn't know of any, but offered to ask a few friends. I gave him my number, and a week later he called to tell me he had someone, but that she'd be hard to get because he was told she wasn't taking on any new clients.

Nothing is impossible. If Prince Harry and his lovely wife Meghan can turn their backs on privileged entitlement, I can get this agent. I was an ordinary human being on a quest for the Holy Grail—put another way, a talented Chicano in search of Quetzalcoatl, the Aztec lord of light. One last ray of hope shot through the utter darkness, and a voice in my head said to go for it, in this city where the inmates had taken over and run the sanatorium. It was just the kind of challenge I needed.

Like my friend from a tribe at the bottom of the Grand Canyon who was the first in his clan to come up and walk the surface of the Earth, I imagined beating out all those entitled sons-a-bitches. . . . Who would even dare but the bravest of us? I wanted to write about people like my surface-earth-walker, people you expect to step right and they go left, people who have held in their tears for a decade, people whose mouths society has duct taped, eyes and ears shut too, and who know the language of silence and terror, whose lives fill a finger thimble of space and have lived in that thimble forever serving others. I wanted to write about people who don't need a scientist to tell them about climate change, who know and practice respect for life, who refuse to let children die of starvation. I wanted to tell a story that your heart would never forget, a heart-touching parable that connected your life to mine, like when you were a child looking up at the stars and wondering if the dragons would come that night, if the prince would ride out of the forest, if the lovers would meet and find each other, if the evil monsters who command global industries killing everything off would be defeated, if the day would come when they'd fall to their knees and beg forgiveness and the world would condemn them to be decapitated.

I guess I shouldn't have asked this publisher's advice. He had a hustle, and it made him enough money to allow him to vacation every two months. He knew that first-time authors would agree to almost anything to get a book contract. He worked his game as skillfully as any oxy or meth dealer. He offered a couple of hundred dollars to the aspiring novelist, and it cost him almost nothing to publish the book. If it made money by word of mouth, then great; if not, so what? What this publisher did was hold the books; not a single one went to bookstores or were distributed. And always, the author was forced to buy his book back; the cost of purchasing his book would be in the thousands. That way, the publisher got paid by the poor author, who was forced to come begging for the return of his intellectual property—actually it amounted to a small ransom.

Despite the publisher's unsavory character, he did give us a contact that was real, and we did get to speak to the movie agent he knew. After driving up in one of those vehicles that is square and reminds you of a London cab, she presented herself as having agented in New York for years and familiar with every studio head by first name. Shortly after sending her my first fifty pages, she accepted us as one of her clients. Norman and I worked each night writing the full 120 pages. We submitted our screenplay to her and she loved it. We signed contracts to have her rep us, and we couldn't have been happier, especially when we knew she had ties to a movie company and had two properties already in production.

Norman and I had agreed we just didn't want to write for the elite; we both believed, and call us backwater or naïve, that helping those who can't help themselves still counted, that compassion and empathy still counted, that those principles were more valuable than any amount of money. We believed that helping kids get an early education was important, that respecting Mexican culture and Indian heritage was supremely at the top of the list, that history written by whites for whites was skewered with such misinformation as to qualify for a Monty Python sketch.

Anyway, we waited and waited to see if the agent landed our screenplay but never got a response. So, Norman started researching her and found out that the movie company she'd set up was a front. I mean, there was *no* movie company. I tried calling the number several times and always got this older woman saying the owner was in Venice and would be back. When I called again, he was in London, and so forth. Then we checked into the two women the agent had advertised on her webpage as having their books in production. We discovered the books were completely contrary to our values. One of the Anglo authors had written about Navajo life, Navajo culture, Navajo dreams and Navajo poverty. A white wealthy woman had chosen to write about impoverished people on Earth. It was another form of pillage and ransacking an indigenous culture, just another white woman, maybe not the cavalry or troopers charging, but by words, which can be powerful weapons when penned by whites for white readers, for New York publishers to make a ton of money when that type of book hits the bestseller list. The other author—holy mackerel!—was even worse: another white woman writing that the

West would have remained savage and godless had not white men come and tamed the savages. I mean, really, are we not over this myth yet? But the lightskins eat it up.

Norman and I sold our screenplay to a Hollywood company out here in Santa Luz. After they read it, we met them one day, had lunch, and by dinner had a check. The agent, a fifty-something divorcée, thin, more bones than skin, with a grandiose opinion of her importance and intelligence, had nothing to do with it, except for one thing. We had not read the tiny print on the contract we had signed with the so-called agent; it said we had to give her a commission. And when our movie came out, she took credit for it and also got some of our royalties.

Norman said maybe walking the surface of the Earth was not such a great deal if you ran into people like her up here. One day over a beer, I asked him again what it was like to never walk the surface of the Earth, to experience the isolation, the removal of all that temptation to own a mortgaged house, a car, to go to school, to smudge out all social contact beyond your own tribe?

He just smiled. A week later Norman went back to live with his people and report to them. I guess, that it's not worth coming up. For myself, well, if you're on the plaza in Santa Luz and you see a dude with white hair down to his shoulders in a ponytail, wearing a Oaxacan cotton vest, Stetson cowboy hat, polished boots (bought in Juarez), western buckle studded with turquoise rocks (Santa Clara Pueblo), a silver wristband and turquoise necklace (San Felipe), diamond earring (Walmart), white shirt with cufflinks, smoking a cigar (7-11) and maybe drinking a margarita, it's me . . . your Santa Luz cowboy.

THE BELLY OF AN AZTEC QUEEN

I remember that once I settled in Santa Luz, the invitations started pouring in. I felt blessed. I packed light and drove out to the Santa Luz airport, boarded a plane and sighed with the greatest relief that I was returning to my old life of writing and speaking engagements. I did promise myself, though, *this time*, I'd behave.

I'd never been one to tiptoe down the middle of anything—wire cutters in one pocket, mini sledge in the other, anything in my way goes down. And this attitude back in the day explained why when I came home, I sat my kids and wife at the kitchen table and said, "Okay, you should know, you all have a new sister. What was supposed to be a one-night stand with a Russian ballerina in a DC hotel turned out to be well . . . a whole hell of a lot of. . . ." (Fill it in).

Once in San Antonio (not sure why, but again it was with a ballet dancer), I asked the bishop if it was wrong for me to have sex with another woman if I was married. He said that as long as I didn't hurt innocent people, as long as I carried my indiscretion to the grave, it was okay. I couldn't have been happier, because I am really good at keeping secrets and really good at fucking on the side. So it worked well for me. I can never thank that bishop enough for his sound advice.

Which brings me to the point of this story. A woman boards the plane with her two daughters and she smiles really big at me. I'm paranoid that . . . that . . . I almost can't bring myself to say it much less think it—that the two girls are mine. Why else the smile?

I've had sex with a lot of wonderful women and not one of them has ever come back for vengeance or accused me of anything. Nor have I ever been the target of a #metoo rage. I don't blame them, and actually, to tell you the truth, I'm as surprised as anyone else at those pristine, clean-cut who parade themselves around as such nice boys and girls—Cosbys, Weinsteins, Trumps, who turned out to be vile rapists and predators. It goes to show you can't tell a man by his skin or wealth. To be honest, I feel I'm not like those pretenders and phonies and fakers that go around in the university halls and classrooms and powerful political positions and then turn out to be Jack the Ripper.

There's nothing wrong with one-nighters. No bullshit, no promises, nothing but fun and sex and go about your business. Okay.

But there I am, sitting in my seat all comfortable, opening my book, *Born a Crime*, when someone touches my shoulder. I turn around. It's one of the little girls who passed with smiley Mom. She asks if she can take a selfie with me, and I say, sure, *no problema*. I probably remind her of her favorite *tío*. We take the selfie, and I go back to reading. A few minutes later, I feel another nudge. I turn and now it's the other little girl, and *she* asks if she can take a selfie. We do, and I return to my reading. Minutes later, *another* little push, and I look up behind me and it's the mother.

Holy of all holies, dear, dear Lord, don't let it be! I've already got nine kids from seven different women. Please, please, Lord, I'll do anything, but don't let it come out of her mouth that I'm the . . .

"Do you remember me?" she asks.

"No-no-no," I reply, "you have the wrong fellow . . . never seen you before. I just got to this country. I am from a faraway island deep in the Amazon jungle."

She grins as if what I said was a cute joke. "You came to my school for young unwed mothers years ago," she starts. "I was in a gang back then and used to let my boyfriend beat on me—I mean, really beat the shit outta me. You were in my class one day, and I was reading something I wrote in my journal. It was a writing class, and I was reading something out loud I wrote about my man beating on me. Like, 'I'm his bitch, he can do anything he wants to me, he owns me. . . .' And all of a sudden, you jump up from the back of the room and start yelling all seriously like, 'Don't you ever let a man hit you. My dad beat my mom . . . and you never let that punk-ass bitch hit you again or I swear I'll go over to your pad and beat the shit out of him.'

"Man, you spun out, no orbit or gravity on your body. You raised up like a Gila monster and flared your dinosaur wings. You were ready to open a can of whoop-ass on him. And you went on and on and you wouldn't stop, for the whole class, about me never letting anyone disrespect me by slamming on me, and you kept on me every class, and it made me change and by the end of the class session—I think it lasted six weeks—I swear, I learned so much self-love from you, so much about what a man can do and what I can do, that I never let another muthafucka lay hands on me.

"I was only thirteen, and you see those two girls, they were in my stomach. I was pregnant with them, and they heard you. I swear to God, they heard your voice all crazy and wild defending their mommy. I know they heard you. They came out and, man, pity the boys or anyone that tries and messes with them. They'll whoop on any ass that disrespects them. I swear, they heard you and listened and learned. That was years ago, as you can see. They're thirteen now, and I always told them about you, and now they see you. You were real to them before. I mean, your voice was. Now they have a face to the voice. Can I take a selfie with you? You're a family member."

Whew, happy to be a family member in *that sense*, man. I'm telling you, everyone on that plane, every single passenger thought I was some kind of big shot celebrity, and I was, but not in the way many of them thought.

Another time recently, one early morning, I was sitting in the Santa Luz airport, a small little architectural gem reminiscent of a 1920's small Midwest bus terminal. But there was nothing small-time about the woman who walked in with her man. Holy moly. Her incredible beauty swept my thinking away. All past turned to ash. It was like the only thing I was conscious of was her. Her hair was so thick and creamy and lustrous, it held a kind of truth, a sort of ancient testament or prophetical thunder, like her hair might be used to conjure spells, black lightning that cracked open the skies and gave light unto the land. Her legs and arms and posture were apportioned so that every movement equaled Vivaldi's finest violin music. Just staring at her I found myself walking alone in a field of sunflowers in northern New Mexico, where the red cliffs meet the blue waters, where the elk and eagle and hawks gather with the deer and mountain lion and wild turkey and do not disturb each other—a balance, a coexistence, even with me in the picture, in tune with God's creation.

I hate to go on so much about this woman. It would be different if I could have her, but no, my dreams are limited. My life is pretty much summed up by the Do Not Disturb sign you hang on the hotel door. Alas, a normal, ordinary life. But that minute I saw her come in, for that minute, it was otherwise: my life had possibilities, it had shine, it gave me what I remember I had in my childhood: the ability to believe in magic.

She sat down with her man next to her, and they didn't talk. I could not take my eyes off her. It was time to board, and I got in line. I handed my boarding pass to the attendant, walked down the breezeway and entered the cabin. To my surprise, when I double-checked the seat number she was sitting next to me.

All I could think of was giving a quiet cry of triumph. *"Wh-hhoooeee!"* a voice inside me celebrated. I glanced around, and behind me two seats down on the left side I saw her husband star-

ing at me with mixed expectations. Like he was going to fuck me
up if I made a move on her. He was in his early thirties, in good
shape, with a crew-cut and a shave as smooth as a baby's butt. I
sensed his alert eyes had seen bad things in Iraq. As he edged bit
by bit toward not liking me, sensing my intentions of flirting with
his wife (I mean who the hell wouldn't!), perhaps even in the
short time I had causing her to divorce him and run away with me
forever, I looked longer than I should at him.

As a true *caballero*, I said, "Sir, would you like to sit here? I
noticed you both in the terminal. . . . You're together, are you not?"

He wasn't expecting this kindness. His features melted, and
he seemed not to know what to say. He muttered a meek thanks
and sidled into the seat that was mine.

It was the seat I had been destined to fill, and perhaps start a
conversation. His wife and I would have had so many things in
common . . . and as she looked into my eyes and discovered her
infallible bond to me—indeed, fated and irreversible connection
to me—and accepted the most profound law of the universe that
she was mine . . . Well, all of that now had fallen to the wayside.

I took his seat a couple of rows back.

Sure enough, a huge man carrying a cage with a cat in it, ut-
tered, "I think I'm sitting there next to you by the window."

"Sure, no problem," I say, and get up and stand in the aisle to
let him in, all two hundred and thirty pounds of him.

I squeezed in next to him, a voice inside my head screaming,
"NO-NO-NO!" He smelled like mothballs, detergent, garlic, skin
and hair grease. I wasn't so sure I could handle it and wondered
what had caused God to abandon me, to exile me to this seat to
suffer a feline allergy that was swelling my throat and watering
my eyes. In the midst of my panic, I heard a voice above, maybe
God's, who knows, he could be this woman, and in this case was,
for I glanced up and there she was.

"Oh, deary," she said, "put Hamilton under your chair and
purr to him."

Before she could utter another syllable, I interjected, "Ma'am, I see you two are married. . . . Please, I insist, take my seat."

I didn't care where she was supposed to sit. She could squat out on the wing, for all I cared. Anywhere else was better than me sitting next to that horrid cat.

She took my seat, I took hers two rows down, next to a young, bouncy kind of fellow, all tendons and jerky youthful energy. He was a coal miner's drop-out son who reminded me of what the pioneers were like: stringy, bobble-headed with straw colored hair sticking up sprocket style. He kept turning to the back to talk with his wife about keeping their little girl in the seat strapped in, and telling his little son to stop screaming and his other boy to settle down. His wife had a country accent, lilting like, "Garner, cain ye beeeehavvvve!"

He was wearing military dungarees and an insulated wooly t-shirt, the kind meth makers in Missouri wear when you see them come out of the shack in the *Winter's Bone* movie. They, too, were skinny and malnourished. I kind of liked him, kind of didn't. I didn't want to like him. I wanted to hold steadfast to my racism, to my bigotry. After all, I had worked hard not to like certain races, and he fit that category: white boy, white trash, white garbage destroying the environment and he doesn't care about anything but his rifles and his pack of Lucky Strikes.

And then, unexpectedly, the flight attendant stopped at our row, leaned in toward him and said, "You can move sir, if you'd like. There's a seat next to her."

"Well, I'll be," he remarked and turned to me. "See, mister, what a good deed'll do? I seen you give up that seat next to that wildflower and then end up over there smashed all up next to that big feller, and then here with me. You thought I'm sort of a kind of firecracker, which I am. . . . Now lookee here—you got the row to yourself to stretch out and enjoy the ride. A good deed won't go unnoticed by the good Lord, *nosirrree*."

With that, he gave me a broad smile and went to sit with his beloved.

I stretched out and begrudgingly admitted to myself that I kind of liked that kid. Goes to show you can never tell what's in the package.

BARRIO DOG

I was thinking while driving to the outskirts of Santa Luz that I never believed in the devil, not really . . . but now I do. The 45th made me a believer in evil. I smiled to myself while driving through the foothills, thinking that someone should make him write a million times, *I will not be an evil man, I will not be an evil man,* on a blackboard after school. He's a bad little dictator. And then for the rest of his life, they should make him pick up dog poop on every street in every neighborhood where people of color live. It would be cool to see that orange-haired loony using his gold golf clubs to scoop it up. Oh well, fantasies get me by. No matter what he said he did for the public good, all his action and words led to his pockets getting lined with our money.

Unlike my Indio buddies. Indians have a funny way of giving you directions. I took this dirt road and then this other one, followed red arrows painted on the trunks of cedars and pinon trees. I headed into the high desert not quite sure I was going in the right direction. I'd been invited to a peyote ceremony. When I would think I turned wrong, there was another red arrow, until finally I got to a place where there were some old trucks parked.

I didn't have anyone to watch my dog, so I brought him with me. I noticed others too didn't have anyone, and I saw these wild Indian pack dogs roaming around. "Uh-oh," I thought, "there's going to be trouble." My dog didn't like other dogs. Sure as hell, there would be a rumble to see who was tougher.

I parked, got my dog out and told him, "Now, look, these rez dogs can be vicious boys, real bad. They'll jump you, they don't fight fair, so watch yourself, and if you get into a spat, remember you're representing us Chicanos. You better not lose. Got it?"

He wagged his tail, tongue out, happily panting to get shit started. I smiled and told him to go on, then, get after it, and he was immediately off looking for trouble.

I had been thinking that this peyote ceremony could help me. I'm rude, impatient, proud, too willful, defiant, and I can go on and on. Initially, I was to take part in the ceremony to help a friend of mine who had gotten bad with the meth. Maybe a vestige of magic would rub off on me and make me a better man. Way out in the distance, I could hear the agonizing howls of a canine battle, the battlefield of growls, yelps and skirmishes so intense and violent I could imagine these huge dust clouds rising over the land. He was doing his duty, and I was proud of him. For an old pound rescue mongrel, he had guts and personality.

I made my way to the main teepee and entered. We started our prayers and chants and passed around a zinc pail full of peyote tea. The fire pit was flaming high, and the leader was singing his prayers long into the night. I was flying way out there among the stars, talking to my spirit animal and seeing friends in bird bodies next to me sailing through the universe. I prayed for all my relations.

Sometime during the night, I felt something nudge my waistline through the teepee cloth and heard aggressive snorts and huffy breaths. A snout pushed against the teepee material, and I realized it was my dog smelling my butt. At some point during the ceremony, as the flames were talking to me, creating all kinds of messages, the flames writing me long letters, the flames standing on a pulpit and preaching to me about who I was, where I came from, who my spirit animal was, taking me along into their universe, where stars and black matter convene in creation of matter and where I was welcomed and embraced and loved, I felt my

damn dog pushing his whole body against my back. I was thinking, "That sonofabitch will do anything to get attention and he
doesn't have any manners. Here I am trying to better myself, trying to pray for a brother in need, when this louse of a dog keeps
trying to burrow under the teepee and screw everything up."

The zinc pail was passed around, and the songs continued.
Each of the twenty or so warriors inside the circle took their turns
singing and speaking. Finally, at some point, the main leader of
the ceremony rose and stood around the circle of us sitting and
chanting, and he leaned low and swept the tent flap open. He went
outside to sing to the moon to call on the power of the night.
That's when I heard a growl that could only be my dog snarling
at the main man.

At that moment I felt like strangling my dog, even with all the
peyote and singing and praying. I looked around at the eyes looking around, each wondering what fool would dare disrespect the
main healer by letting his dog threaten him. I peeked back with
an innocent look at the others, with an inquisitive look that meant
I was wondering who would dare do this too. I was pretending the
whole time I didn't know anything about any dog and that the
dog in question should be skinned and roasted on a spit and its
owner flayed with a cactus whip.

The elder healer entered again and looked around, none too
happy at the encounter with the rabid creature. I acted like I had
no knowledge of any of it. But again, the snout pushing and jab-
bing at my butt, the loud sniffs, the grunts and growls behind me
made me sing even louder to hide the sounds of this uninvited in-
truder. At the same time that I was embarrassed, I was also proud
that this crazy dog would have such alliance and loyalty, making
sure I was around and safe. Really, all he wanted was to be by me.

When the sun rose, the ceremony ended, and we all came out
and stretched. We were hungry and headed for the open-air shed,
under which were tables filled with all kinds of food—freshly
butchered goat meat, tortillas, chili, stews and *pozole*. Any nor-

mal dog smelling these delicious foods would be over there, as many were, but not mine. He came right up to me. I looked around at the others, who were now staring at me, glaring, saying, "Oh, so you're the idiot who owns that devil mutt."

Pretending I wasn't, I shooed my dog away. Of course, he didn't budge, just barked, wagged his tail, ran around me and jumped up, until I finally admitted without a word that he was mine.

I didn't have the heart to sit and eat with the rest of my brothers and sisters. So, I called him to me. We hugged, and I petted him, and we both walked to the truck. He leaped into the back. We drove off. None of the rez dogs followed us out. They all stood and watched, afraid they'd get another ass-whipping. As we drove off, he was standing on all fours in the truck bed, staring at them like he had done his duty and taught them a lesson.

The Indians in the shed also looked at me as I was driving away, but it wasn't because I had proven my courage and bravery. It was because I had prayed for one of theirs. Suddenly, they waved me back, and I turned my truck around and got out. They invited me to join them in eating what turned out to be the best mutton I ever tasted. They even threw some to my dog and started laughing about how they too heard the crazy dog sniffing at the teepee hem. The whole time they were really laughing to themselves despite keeping their faces rock stern—gotta love these homeboys.

In the end, the peyote, the fire and the whole experience had healed something in me. It connected me to something deep down that I really needed.

THE TREMBLING

If I don't have to, I rarely talk about my past, riddled as it is with upheaval and drunkenness and parental violence and drug addiction, all of which have left an indelible mark on me, even though I tend to pretend otherwise.

There's a prison just outside of Santa Luz, and my friend Rascal invited me to help him film a writing workshop there. He was trying to prove that sign language, not ASL, but prison sign language, was a legitimate language unique to prisoners and understood by them all over the world. I knew that. I had seen Chinese cons signing to African cons, Chicanos to Bloods and Crips—it was their language. Secret codes shared by the imprisoned.

It was an opportunity for me to see what it was like in prison. I had some friends doing time. Who doesn't, these days, right? I mean it's odd if you don't have a family member locked up or an extended family member held hostage by the legal system, right?

It's like the AIDS epidemic. At first no one would admit they knew anyone who had it because of shame, or perhaps others might think you were gay or something. But then, when it became okay to know them, it turned out we all had friends with AIDS, mostly from using dirty needles.

Peter Jennings, the newsman, was coming inside with us to film the experiment. Let me point out now, right before we go any further, this story is not about the legitimacy of hand-sign language among the imprisoned and oppressed of the world, but about what happened to me while I was inside helping Rascal out.

This story is not so much about the sign language they used. They couldn't read a Shakespearean poem but they could sign it to their wives on camera, they could sign any poem, an entire novel, a whole memoir, but they could not read one. This story's not about that either.

It's about the trembling in my body. The trembling that shook inside me every time I tried to hug someone I loved, every time I tried to embrace someone. The shaking put up a wall, a seismic barrier that kept me distant and feeling like there was something wrong with me.

Sure, I went to see a couple of counselors about it, even a therapist and a psychiatrist. I felt like I could not really love anyone, like something had been hammered out of me a long time ago. It was like someone had staked down a tent, the kind you see on civil war battlefields, and no one was allowed to go into this tent . . . because someone was dying in there, someone was sick and whatever he had you might also get, so better not go in there. That's what that trembling was like in me: a sick man on a cot in there and no one allowed to visit him.

When I got married and my baby boy was born, the first time I held him, I felt that shaking. Who put that in me? I wondered. Who would do that, and what was it? Right through the rib cage, originating in the heart (I guess), the shakes and tremors spread up through the arm bones to the shoulders and down to my loins and kneecaps and thighs. . . . It was a shaking so slight, something like a light breeze blowing the feathery pappus off a dandelion flower, the kind you pick as a child and blow to see them scatter in the air. In me they scattered, but like embers burning me, singeing me, scabbing me—and it hurt. I'd go around acting normal, I was not.

It happened again with my second baby. I couldn't hold him without feeling the tremor inside me. My wife finally admitted to me that ever since the first time she hugged me, she felt something go from me to her, like some slow-moving, frightened snake exiting my chest and swerving into her skin and sliding between her ribs—it was not a good feeling.

The shaking was so small, like one of those monks that hits a bronze cymbal and then meditates, except I imagined they used their breath to blow the cymbal, and the sound would be such that only bats might hear it. That's how it was. I don't know if it meant I was a violent man waiting to crack, if I was a serial killer, if the tension stressed me out when it was time for me to show a little love to someone. Maybe it was a sign that I was about to explode—snap, shatter reality as I and the ones I loved knew it.

One doctor asked if I ever had heart problems.

"No, never. I can kick out a 3-mile run."

Another asked if I had ever been molested. No.

The answer finally came when I was in that prison helping Rascal, after those writing workshops he was facilitating. An old California Indian of some kind, trying to get his tribe recognized by the United States government, invited us to do a sweat ceremony. The newsman Jennings freaked out. He didn't know what a sweat ceremony was and he loaded up his camera crew and took off. But a couple of the women working for the news company decided they'd stay.

After we had finished clearing the library and saying goodbye to the inmates, the two women, Rascal and I went around the buildings to another one set off by itself in the back. We got undressed in a shower room and put on some shorts. The old native dude said the women could not come in, but they could wait for us by the huge fire pit, where there was a place for them to sit. They seemed cool with it.

We were led into a teepee along with some of the inmates and we sat down in a circle around a small pile of red-hot rocks. Those in the know started singing and chanting. One of the inmates, a tall former basketball player from El Paso, started crying, laid down on the ground and grabbed my hand like I was his mother or something. I was okay with that. The other homey, the East-Los *vato*, curled up behind me in a fetal position and cried into the dirt.

The fire keeper con kept going in and out, bringing in more red-hot stones, making it hotter, unbearably hotter. When the pile of stones was high enough, we sat in utter darkness. We couldn't see anyone, only heard voices, many voices, all singing and gasping and roaring and crying. There were groans and more groans of pain and anguish and more singing. And I'm like thinking, "Enough, man, enough already, I'm about to pass out, I can't take anymore!" And just as I was about to pass out, a middle-aged white dude screamed out that he had to leave or he'd die. So, the native leader opened the tent flap to let him out. In the light that shone in from the flap, I could see all these indigenous convicts, three people deep and in a circle, all hugging each other and cradling each other, helping each other through the pain and sorrow of their lives.

I'd never seen anything like that: so many men, supposedly hardened criminals, embracing each other in pain and joy and singing each other's pain to peace. I'd never seen a man surrender so helplessly his manhood and embrace his vulnerable side. For a moment, in the light, I saw them as young boys, as if they, and I, were all caught in a terrible catastrophe. We needed to hold on to each other to survive the end of our world as we knew it. Arms and legs and torsos were entangled, heads lolled, long hair fell across faces and shoulders, and that's when something happened to me.

I scooted closer to the fire pit, as close as I could, took the gourd ladle from the zinc pail and drank. I started singing a hymn I'd learned in church when I was a choir boy: *"Bendito, bendito, bendito sea Dios. Los ángeles cantan y alaban a Dios. Bendito, bendito, bendito sea Dios. . . ."*

I don't know where I got the strength to endure the heat, but I sang, and everyone in the teepee paid homage to my strength by grunting and crying out loud "*ho/ho/ho . . .*"

Afterwards, we all came out and stood in a big circle, and they gave us each a gift from their tribe: a bracelet, a belt, a ring, a talisman. One thing I never knew, and which I saw that day, was that some of the *indios* were white. I didn't know there were white Indians, and black and Asian Indians also, all kinds of indigenous from various tribes around the world were there giving me and the others gifts, including the women, until we could hardly carry them. There were so many.

When I left the prison that day, my son was waiting outside in the parking lot to pick me up. I approached him, grabbed him and hugged him, and the trembling was gone.

Even he noticed it and said, "No trembles, Pop?" He was smiling broadly.

I'll never understand why or how, but there must have been a healing that took place in that sweat. A soul healing.

BEEHIVE

The tattoo covered his arms, legs, chest and stomach. He was in the Santa Luz county jail, busted for selling weed. He'd been in a lot of times. At age eighteen, he had spent more than half of his life behind bars of one sort or another. Institutionalized was the word used in all the official papers, the court papers, the probation papers, and in truth the label meant nothing. It was just a way to justify paying a lot of people for keeping young adults like him behind bars or in juvey halls or detention centers. A lot of people made their living off kids like him, a good living—nice car, nice apartment, nice clothes, eating at good restaurants, taking vacations—all off guys like him. He really was just another homeless Chicano kid without an education and no family, no parents. These kids were out there doing whatever they needed to get drugs or alcohol, scamming, petty thievery, burglaries, breaking into cars, stealing stuff to sell to their front.

His name was Dominic, and he loved selling weed. He made a decent living off it when he was free to wheel and deal. Every morning in his cell, he took out his needle and scissors and syringe, cut pieces of his bed sheet, laid out the leaf-size cuttings, plunged the needle into his arm, extracted the blood and squeezed it onto one of the leaves. Once he had enough dried pieces, he massaged them with toothpaste and carefully wrapped them around a piece of toilet paper he made wet. He then dried it until it was a hardened stem and wrapped the red pieces of sheeting around and around, shaping and forming them into a perfect rose.

Everyone knew them as Dominic's roses. And every convict in
the cell pod wanted one. After drying them, he'd pull threads
from his sheet and wrap the petals around the stem, and he'd have
his rose.

There was a waiting list for his roses. He'd run his finger
down the list and, after locating the next customer's name, he'd
walk down the tier and exchange the rose for a little baggie of
heroin or coke. Then Dominic would return to his cell, where he
mixed the drugs in his bottle cap, inserted the ingredients into the
syringe and then into his vein. It was the best way to pass time
until his sentence was up and he was free again.

That was the business of the day, every day. It was routine,
until the day one of the guys who was standing at the end of the
tier hand-signing to his girlfriend told him there was a chick
passed out on the bus bench. She didn't look too bad, and maybe
Dominic could get her to talk to him.

He went to the window, looked down on the street corner,
where a group of whores were gathered, signing up to their guys
on other floors below and above. Dominic signed to them to wake
the chick on the bus bench up. They roused her, pointed to him,
and he signed asking her name. She didn't respond because she
didn't know prisoner sign language. So he signed to the whores
to translate for him. And they did, asking her what she was doing
on the bus bench. She flipped him off, walked away and was
gone. Oh well, it was worth a try. He went back to his cell, in-
jected his arm and nodded off on the heroin. Forget about her.

The rain woke him the next morning before breakfast time.
He strolled down to the window to look at the rain and there, to
his surprise, she was again, sleeping on the bench in the rain.

He went back to his cell, cut out a cardboard flap from a box
he had under his bed, traced his hand on it and smeared it with
white toothpaste. He tied a popsicle stick to the end of it. It looked
like a clown's hand. The rain had stopped. He carried his cut out
it to the window, stuck his arm out and started waving it and

whistling. Finally, he got her attention, and she looked up and waved back at him.

He pointed, hand signing to her to go next door to the bail bondsman. When she did, a woman came out and looked up and understood. She knew Dominic; he had made roses for her for bail. She read his signals and told the girl who he was and that he wanted to know her name. He also wanted to know why she was sleeping on the bench.

Over time, the girls on the corner taught her—Melanie was her name—to sign, and soon every morning Melanie and Dominic would carry on long conversations in prison sign language. He found out she lived with her grandparents. She had dropped out of school and she'd spend every afternoon smoking meth in the city flood channels or parks. Afterward, her father, drunk and violent, would look for her at her grandparents' house. She didn't feel safe there and decided to sleep on the bench outside the prison walls.

Dominic also told Melanie about himself, that his parents were absent, he lived mostly by himself except when he had a girl, he sold weed and was doing nine months for selling. He confessed that he liked heroin and did it daily, financed from the proceeds of selling his roses.

They became good friends and overtime, along with the prostitutes on the corner, he taught her how to move her fingers, how to create the street alphabet and make words and sentences by flashing her hands and fingers in certain motions. That's how they were able to communicate on various topics: family history, drug use, who knew who in the drug game, whatever interested them. This was how it went for weeks, until one day she failed to show up. Every day after that, Dominic stood at the window and waited. He doubled and tripled his roses output and sent them to the address she had given him, her grandparents'. Sometimes he fell into a reverie of sorts and made roses all day until he grew weak and anemic from drawing so much blood.

After a long period of absence, when Melanie finally returned, she told him she'd gone back to stay with friends and did
drugs every day. But, finally, she was done with it. She told him
that in order for them to be lovers, he had to stop using heroin.
Otherwise, she would never come back again.

Disagree and argue as Dominic might, he had to give in because he loved Melanie. He convinced her to get off meth and
talked her into going back to school. He, in turn, quit shooting
heroin and began to read the Bible every day. Not watching TV
made his nights much longer, but time seemed to fly when he was
absorbed in reading Scripture. In fact, to his surprise, he began to
enjoy reading the Holy Book, not for the sake of being saved or
redeemed, but because he decided it was actually a good story,
gory and violent and bloody, which he liked.

Every morning, Dominic rose happily to engage in hand jive
with his beloved, who was now looking good. She saved her
money, bought new clothes and was getting top grades in school.
She shared all the gossip with him—who got busted, who was
turning tricks, the new pimps and drug dealers, what cops were
crooked, the judges on the take. . . . She'd ask if he knew so and
so who was locked up with him, because she knew their girl-
friends, who were fucking other guys. She shared all the juicy
and scandalous morsels of rumor and savored them with him in
their hand talks. Melanie would sit on the bench and sign for
hours, sometimes lying down. And he would tell her stories until
she fell asleep, stretched out on the concrete and wooden bus
bench. She'd ask if he thought there was life up there in the stars.
They'd talk about it, about the dreams and stars and childhood
fantasies and frights, their fears, hopes, future plans, which in-
cluded them getting married, buying a house, getting good jobs
and having kids.

One day, Melanie showed up with her grandparents. They
wanted to meet him and thank him for helping their granddaughter change and stay in school. Also, they wanted to tell him

the roses were coming in and filling up their house. They'd soon have to move, there were so many roses. They smiled grandly at this, and she translated for them. The grandparents threw big warm embraces to him up in his cell as they left to return home.

After the visit from her grandparents, Melanie went back to her usual routine. Even when it snowed, she would be there for all the commuters to see, flashing her love signs to her man. When it rained, she sat there catching drops with her mouth or dancing in the puddles while he watched and laughed and clapped. At night, he would watch her sleep, chase away bums and addicts and threaten homeless people to leave her alone. When fellow inmates were released, he watched as they crossed the street and handed her an armful of roses.

She would cry with joy or out of sadness. No one had ever been so kind to her.

After six and a half months of falling deeply in love, Melanie showed up one day with eyes swollen from crying and her cheeks wan. She had been up all night. When he asked what the problem was, she shook her head and looked down.

"Did you relapse? Did you use again? Did your father do something to you, rape you, molest you? Did an old boyfriend come back into your life?"

It was no to all the questions.

"Then what?"

She signed up to him the news that she had been offered a scholarship to a university in Kansas. It would be a free ride: dorm, food, everything. She could become the nurse she had dreamed of. But she said she would not leave, she loved him so much. She'd rather die than leave him there.

However, when she came back the following morning, he did not show. She signed up to all the black brothers and the Chicanos to please wake him up or bring him to the window. But all they could do was relay her messages to him while he lay on his bunk staring at the ceiling.

Melanie was his first and only real love, but that did not stop Dominic from making his decision. On the fifth day, he went to the window and found Melanie standing down there half-starved, tears flowing. He signed that he was fine, that he needed time to think. He told her that she had to go, and he would find her when he was released. What followed were days full of Melanie crying and fighting against his wishes. Dominic ordered her to go and get her education, promising that he would follow.

Months later, when his release date came, carrying his Bible, he took a bus down to her house on West Santa Fe Street. Her grandfather offered him a beer and they sat down on the porch, not saying much, just staring out on the street at nothing.

Dominic turned and asked, "May I have permission to see Melanie's room?"

Dominic walked into her bedroom, sat down and looked around. The entire room—walls, door, bathroom and bed, except for passageways—was covered in roses.

Every drop of blood had come from his heart to make this garden. It was what his heart in love with a beautiful homegirl looked like.

AHS A-CUMMINS

For my birthday I decided to treat myself to a class and I signed up at St. James College in Santa Luz. I didn't realize so many of my past acquaintances, born and raised in Santa Luz, were attending the college. We greeted each other where we had left off years ago, "Hallo, hallooooo," kind of making fun of the way Gringos think we talk.

But, kidding aside, to get on with my paper here, if they hadn't made it into such a big deal, nothing would have happened. My professor handed out the lesson plan with a novel I had to read. I started reading and realized it was one of *those* novels: white woman writes novel about Mexicans. Some publicist or agent or publisher, or all three, decided we needed saving. The book had its celebrity advocate; Oprah invited a person who I call Mouth-Grinder#1 to support the book and author and had the meeting televised. They blew it way out of proportion: this was the novel for all time that would redeem our poor insufficient writers and poets who didn't have the capacity to write our own stories but needed instead to rely on the 14-karat wits of a white woman who touristed down in Mexico and looked at Mexicans like they were a strange species in a zoo. (Mouth-Grinder#1 is like those monkeys tied to the owner by a neck chain and their job is to hold out a tin cup to collect donations as the organ grinder plays on.)

But this time the organ grinder didn't get out of bed and the monkey escaped back to the jungle and their publicity machine broke down, and all hell broke loose. Or as my grandpa used to say, "Someone left a little rock in the beans."

So here is the part, Professor Torrez, where I must beg, please, to be excused from the conventional paper. I know the assignment. I went to class regularly and on time, and I know I am accountable for turning in a paper on the assignment you gave for our final grade and final exam.

But I got lost. Partly because I fell in love with this blond chick in my class. You've seen her, she sits right up front where I can only guess how you've dreamed of her when those beautiful legs stretch out in front of you. How do you bear the temptation? Oh, my gawd, the strain. How can you tame your temptation, not leap on her, kiss her kneecaps, devour her thighs and calves with your tongue? I mean this. She does this to me, makes me feel like I go out of myself and could possibly do things completely contrary to my nature. When I see her sitting in class, I feel like I've bit into a really tart lemon and find myself puckering my lips and twisting my features up. It's ridiculous, I know, but love is . . . blah blah blah . . . you know.

Back to my research paper and begging you not to flunk me. I'm really hoping to give you the best paper you ever received, but in route to writing it for you, I got sucked up and chewed and swallowed by this controversy about a white woman writing a book about our immigrant dilemma and her supposed right to do so at the expense of publishers dismissing so many of our own writers, many of whom, unlike her from her entitled background, have suffered the immigrant experience.

I only took this sociology class because of the blond-haired, blue-eyed chick. That day standing in the registration line in the gym, she was in front of me, and I overheard her ask for the class and then watched her fill out the card. I followed suit. I was crazy about her. And later in class when you said write me a paper on how social groups form, the essential grouping dynamics of people and what makes them come together under certain ideological passions, I never thought I'd get lobbed right into a three-ring circus with warring factions over immigration policy and what kind of country we want to be.

Are you kidding me? I just wanted to get laid by a beautiful white girl with the finest little booty you ever saw. Jeez, now I might get flunked just because I followed my biological yearnings. Not fair, not fair at all. But I have to stay tough, I'm the first one in my family that has had the opportunity to go to school, first one. That's huge in my immigrant *familia*.

My adolescent intentions aside, I found myself sucked down Dorothy's rabbit hole (remember there's no place like home . . . ?) into a weird land of sensuous Oz, bristling with literary rancor over the exploitation of a white author's novel and the white publishing industry so near-sighted it can't see past bewitching whiteness.

And if it wasn't for it being the final exam, I could've blown it off, got down to more important things, like getting her to bed, taking her out to eat, hike, browse bookstores; little wine and bingo, *plop,* in the sack—sure as fish bait on a hook. Ugh, now the assignment has really got me messed up.

Social marketing of information? And who controls the message, the intent of the message? I thought it would be easy enough to fire up Google, check out some articles and write something, turn my paper in and be done, get my grade and finally take my beautiful blue eyed girl fishing up at Chama.

But then, as happens in life to me more than it should, when I googled under sociology and populations and groupings, I stepped right into a literary hornet's nest, a quicksand of cultural appropriation by this white female writer who had just published a novel on Mexican asylum seekers and immigrants. White-owned bookstores hailed her as our messiah, booked her coast to coast. From indigenous/Chicana/Chicano quarters in America (God bless those brave voices), it stirred up a maelstrom of criticism on the book's lack of anything that pertained to reality. Pure, unadulterated stereotypical soap-opera biases page after page. Somebody was *again* (sigh) making us up, viewing our Chicano culture through the clouded eyepiece of the Eurocentric monocle.

But white women loved it. White readers hailed it as the best writing. It became a best seller. The story fit snugly into their skewered perception of Latinos. And the publishers couldn't care less who they were stigmatizing, as long as the loot was coming in. They were hard selling the book like it was pure cocaine, hand over hand on street corners, gasping during shift change, lugging sacks of dinero to the banks, a veritable "Scarface" line.

But really, Professor, who cares whether this outsider appropriated our culture, who cares if she tweaked and twisted the Mexican character into a subhuman degenerate to keep the white reader breathless in New Hampshire or Vermont and on edge about the next violent scene or drug dealer. It's what the literary soap opera is all about: *shootembangabangup* drama.

So, I finally get around to reading it, and by this time my babe Gloria and I are like a couple, and I'm telling my blond goddess as we drive over to her house the premise of my paper, that groups are driven to gather and network based on simple pleasures. Water runs downhill, so do we. We go for what's easiest, most comforting, no heroes among us anymore. We all click up, each of us has our crew, we are part of the group because it's safe and pleasurable.

I forced myself to focus on the controversy, use it as an example, illustrate it with facts, but when I saw her body in the kitchen doorway—holy miserable me—maintaining my focus was harder than stopping a runaway train. I did manage to sit her down at the kitchen table and explain the literary dust-storm surrounding this white woman from a privileged background writing about immigrants. But the truth is . . . I had to leave . . . because of sex, all I could think about was sex.

So, I'm up and out of there. A little later at Dunkin Donuts to study, I start thinking: it comes down to money. Who makes the money. Who gets to walk away writing about Latinx misery and oppression? All you have to do to sell your words and write a bestseller on immigration, in the author's words, is spend a little time "traversing the borderlands, visiting orphanages and volunteering at a soup kitchen for migrants."

One Chicana writer fired a shot over the bow, with this: ". . . she identified the Gringo appetite for Mexican pain and found a way to exploit it." I later read this part to my blond goddess, and it wasn't quite enough to unlock her chastity belt. She didn't like to get involved with racial politics, especially since the topic was about my people. But there was one thing she mentioned that made me think: where were the protests of Latino writers whose books have been published by these large commercial publishers? No one has heard from them. There's nothing like corporate allegiance—being a company writer is a good career move.

A few days later, Gloria and I go down to the Railyard Brewery with friends. It's west of the plaza, west Santa Luz, and as I looked around the table, it struck me that I was the only one with a white girl. All my white friends were dating Chicanas. White guys all with Chicanas. Why don't they stay within their race? Why do white guys like Chicanas? Well, the whole gathering that night confused me even more, but it didn't stop me from getting to work on my paper. "Get it done get it done get it done" was the mantra in my head, beating drums at all hours of the day and night.

I went down to the school library to work on my paper and found myself smiling, fascinated by a few white girls I passed on the way. After hours of grueling research and writing, I figured I had enough material to get going, but later that night, instead of diving into the final write on my paper, I found myself thinking more about my place in this city called "Santa Luz Exotic," when it should be called—"City of Divisions," "City of Indifference," "City where the rich toss the Chicanos off to the margins," "City where the rich buy up everything," "City where rents are no longer affordable," "City where outsiders claim to rewrite the history of my city."

I googled Bowels, Esmeralda and Garcia, writers I liked, to see if they had anything on Chicano cities taken over by whites—trust funders, you know, and their gentrification crap. Hadn't a long history of colonialism been enough? Wasn't the rape and pillaging and destruction of my culture enough? Now, instead of infected blankets, guns and swords, they come at us with words and money? They cloak their false Samaritan phrasing in sweet mannerisms, liberal bullshit, like "I wanna help you," "I'm here as your brother to save you."

Hadn't the Inquisition done enough? Hadn't a hundred years of racial oppression been enough? Now, they resort to using publishers and million-dollar-marketing campaigns to convince the book buying public that our stories are more legit and more authentic coming from a white writer?

I could not believe the publishers were so out of touch, or that they could manipulate public opinion so much, turning what was real into an unreal comical version of the real thing. I guessed when a lot of corporate mouthpieces or company writers come out strapped with a book at their hip ready for an OK Corral shootout with anyone in their way, supporting a book, they operate under the pack mentality—tell people the moon is purple enough times, they'll believe it. It's like those cults, you know, when people believe their leader is a god. Some people must believe corporations are gods. Institutions hate change; the status quo is their bread and butter. You come in, they give you a position and an office, you do as they say, you get in line, you dump your brains at the nearest doorway trashcan and stop thinking.

(Professor, I took this out thinking you might be offended by it. Then I put it back in to show what I took out.) Institutions can only exist as long as loyalty to them is enforced. Take away the institution—universities, government agencies—and the ordinary employees vanish. Havoc reigns in the world. They are only as much and as real as the institution. Take a look at Madoff's son hurling himself out of a skyscraper window—he was money, money was him and when it was gone, he was gone. Institutions only hire you based on their belief that you will put it over your own desires, that its commands will be obeyed at all costs, that you agree that you don't matter, your opinions don't matter except in how they need you to do what they need, to execute their plans and be predictable. . . . So it's no wonder you hate free thinkers.

I read the book, and at this point in my letter to you asking for mercy and a good grade, I have to admit I don't believe anyone has the right to tell anyone else what they can write or not write. And if she banks a little bread, all the better. (I heard she's made millions depicting Mexicans as drug dealers and cowards). A lot of Chicano and Chicana writers are just jealous—they want the attention of big NYC publishers, they want the millions that writing what pleases them can award them, an emotion as old as cavemen picking their nose. *Envidia.* They begrudge this young author the right to write whatever she wants, and maybe in some cases, write it even better than them. That could be it, you know. I'm not pissed that they ganged up on her, but that our Raza, you know, we're followers: one person does it, the rest follow. We're like that, tribal, community-orientated, we like ganging up on people, those brave loners out there. To see who's writing on who, who is being left out, who is in, to see the gang-mentality at work, makes for an entertaining pastime.

There were questions I couldn't answer. I just wasn't into the whole literary scene. There's that San Miguel de Allende crowd down there who whine and complain about their toenails they can afford or can't. Never seen such grown-up babies posing as cultural scribes, on-call for Oprah or NPR at the drop of a denture. Social media and online gossip are filled with their comments.

I had come upon the controversy at the end and by accident. I read articles from major newspapers and online mags with the eagerness of a kid who didn't know much. It mattered because outside of literature, even the bozo in the White House, that ugly white dude, was pushing his racist agenda, really causing good people to start chanting, "You don't belong here." But I was determined to get a good grade and not end up at day's end like one of those old ladies at home in bed under doctor's orders for ovarian cancer, poisoned by Los Alamos labs, where she worked as a cleaning lady for decades.

Okay, so let's start this paper with this sentence: White women writers can write for black writers, for Chicano and Mexican writers, for Native and indigenous writers, and feel they have the right. No, maybe not. But if they can write for refugees and asylum seekers, if they can write for Mexicans, why not the rest?

I crossed the quad, adjusting my ear buds and nodding to the music of Nipsey Hussle. I don't quite understand why anyone would be afraid to speak out, even though I rarely do. And I do realize my own naivety, my lack of literary expertise. I never read, so this new subject you (Professor) gave me, this task finds me in such a mess in trying to figure out what the hell it means. It has now dwindled down to this simple question: Do whites have the right to write about Mexican culture, Mexican immigrants, Mexican strife and life and dreams and hopes, especially whites who get paid a lot for doing it when there are literally dozens of Mexican writers and Hispanic writers who can do it, but the publishers won't contract them because they prefer whites.

I keep feeling that difference wherever I walk. The dividing line is everywhere, and the whites keep moving the goal post to suit their needs, which is almost always because they want more money, always wanting more, *los pinches babosos*, devising new tactics to get more money, more property, more power over the Chicanos.

At the store, at the apartment complex, at the plaza, at the gym, at the park, I feel their looks say you don't belong. I wonder why they need to do this, why they come into a city where generations of my Raza have lived and died and call it theirs because they have money and can remove us to the outskirts of the city because they have paid off political cowards. They take our historic plaza and give it a facelift for tourists and make it their version of what I am supposed to be.

Old Ms. Winfrey liked the book. She endorsed it, saying it woke her up. She must have been on some serious Quaaludes. My question to her is, "If it woke you up, where the hell have you been—I mean, what planet?" Asylum seekers and immigrant families have been in the news almost daily for years, and you just woke up to that? And it takes a cheap *narconovela* to suddenly stir your mind to the fact that there's so much trauma committed against innocent immigrant families?

I know, I'm too naïve, went to Highland High and into St. James before you could say enchilada. My parent's cautionary sense of peril led me to go to school as "the only way you'll break out of this barrio and make a decent life for yourself." BS, of course, since everyone knows administrators are all on the take. My parents forgot to mention and explain why the city I was born in has been given a makeover, redefined as a city for rich whites, keeping most of the street names in Spanish to make it more quaint, to give it an exotic Spanish air, outfitted with the whole rigmarole: Stetson cowboy hats and Frida Khalo skirts and turquoise beaded cowboy boots. It's a city gentrified by trust funders, people with .com money, Silicon Valley white hippies who sold their computer chip companies and came to Santa Luz to do yoga on their patio while watching their Chicano gardeners and maids sweat in the sun for minimum wage. They ummm to the distant rhythm of hedge-trimmers and later read novels about immigrant families written by the Gringos.

What also bothered me was that the controversy offered little good to general start-up readers like me. They looked foolish, like classroom kids fighting for seats up front. When I read their words, I felt a kind of stomach pain, as if the words of these supporters of Latinx literature written by white ladies were clothed in a veneer of falsehood. I couldn't pick anything out specifically, but I felt it, their beguilement carried on the page ever so carefully and generously, like a servant carrying a tray laden with wine glasses, shimmering with wine that has been poisoned, careful not to spill a drop.

The whole thing has made my head spin like some cat just turning into the wrong alley where there are wild dogs. This book is the prime example of how to get over on the reading public by pretending this white author has a right to tell our story, to vacation in Mexico and call it research, to interview immigrants on both sides and call it an experience that swallows you and proves you know us enough to write our dreams and injustices down.

But I have to say, the whole bantering, barking and hawking that sells this book feels like an evangelical tent meeting, where snake handling is the proof of faith, and the raspy, male preacher up there, sweating like a South Carolina whore on a paddle wheel boat, prim and mannered, promises salvation for a little money in the basket. It's like the holy water in the church fountain being spiked with ecstasy. And I feel like I'm almost ready to leap up and clap and kick my heels and start talking in tongues, talking in other people's cultural dialects, telling them what I know, telling them, "Follow me, and I will tell your story through the eyes of a chosen one." And when that basket is passed, it makes the preacher (writer) willing to say anything, go on tour and tolerate the naysayers, because with that money, he goes on to his next evangelical meeting down the road, maybe to tell a story about black slavery and how it felt.

If you want to know the truth, Profe, it's about mind control. You know, either that or a lot of people are smoking powerful ganja. ¿Me entiendes? The rumor rags are heating up—gossip troughs have the usual literary voices guzzling at them. I realize by their blind and absolute defense that they could be commending pedophilia and it wouldn't matter to them; they just want to defend this woman. Mouth Grinders will find a way to advocate the righteousness of it, like saying, pedophilia helps us immigrant kids, its best for us.

For someone not part of the day-to-day dribble that pours out of the publishing industry on what books are great or not, it means nothing. You have to love books, and I do, but I don't read, although I now want to read more, but I don't care for the attacks on this writer. So what? She misfired. So what she got it wrong? It's not the end of the world, *pendejos* (not you, Profe, I'm just talking).

The problem is the publishers: they should publish more Chicanos/as, more Latinx *plebe*. Catch up, *putos*, there's so many more views out here and such great literature on the immigrant experience. You don't have to have a white woman teaspoon it out to mainstream America. She's just another bystander trying to pay the rent, a spectator who writes on Monday what happened on Sunday.

I have to tell you again, Profe: this letter is to please ask you to give me a passing grade and to tell you I'm in love with this blondie. It's her fault I didn't do it right. She distracts me with her laughter, the way her tongue and lips shine with saliva, the way her eyes kind of look around but don't see anything, the way her thighs and butt smoothly merge into each other like God is holding out his hand saying, "Come to me, Julio."

The things that a person will do for money, *verdad*? And in my case, for love.

The industry flipped all the selective switches for this writer chick, turning all the wheels to recruit Latina writers to gush and blush on what a great novel it is. I'm like, what? (In my head I'm thinking maybe these Latina writers will tell me I can walk on water or become invisible to *la Migra*.) Man, these well-ironed, wrinkle-free literary linens just shook out their perfumed opinions and promoted a book by a white woman about us Chicanos and Mexicans and the ongoing tragedies we suffer at the border: in coming north, in living violence-free, in asking for a little respect and the right to life. But these Publisher Girls and Winfrey are cheerleading her. What's next, a self-help book by Bill Gates on the Joys of Poverty?

I read and go over again that this white lady has written the book that finally describes my life? It tells it in a way that a thousand other Mexican authors and poets aren't qualified to because we don't have that cleanliness that publishers look for, we don't have the ice cream cart and summertime ice cream smiley temperament, we don't have the white sensibility that colors and infuses our text so other white men and women can sip their wine in Santa Monica and fold legs under their butts and read our story written by a woman chosen by God, elected by the Inquisitors, the New York Literati.

As for the do-good liberals, those who can't stand the taint of racism and wish it didn't exist—oh, they secretly relish it. They want to wash away our differences, to wish them gone, to believe for a second that white people haven't forever been appropriating our culture and experiences and turning them into spiteful and deliriously laughable movies and TV episodes. . . . Then this maiden comes along on a white horse, the fairy godmother, with a wand, who tells us things will be fine, "I am here, I will speak for you." *No hombre, es puro pedo.*

Well, well, well. I wonder what these rich pale skins would be doing if they weren't always sticking their noses in our culture? Traveling? Shopping? Relaxing poolside? Having tea? I suppose to make your irreverent non-person relevant you have to do something. It seems everyone has squatter's rights these days. As if one orange-haired puke-basket wasn't enough, we have another form of pushing your weight around to get what you want. "My way or no way," the publishers seem to say when it comes to Chicano and Mexican immigrant literature. I have the power, the distribution forces at my disposal to deploy an army of newspaper editors and media chieftains to destroy your opinion. We want to hear the choir, our choir, talk about how great this book is. The women we've lavished with advances, who's books we've promoted, will sing out the praises that will sell this book. We don't need an authentic brown woman—no Chicanas, replicas will do, dolls if you will, that look like Chicanas, but speak for us.

They disguise her as one of us and unleash the army of public relation squads to control the narrative on how this white woman novelist is one of us. Don't mention she lives a life of privilege. Line up the artillery, set loose the jets, lob the bombs into every major online news source, Sunday book section and cable outlet and give the public the overriding avalanche that this book is what Mexicans want, what Latinos need, that she is the savior. Blockade and set up check points to make sure no other voices get in. A famous Chicana is quoted as saying to promote the book, "It's written in a form that will engage people, not just the choir, but people who might think differently. We're always looking for the great American story, and this is the great story of the Americas, at a time in which borders are blurred."

Now, that's some heavy butt-slapping and cheek kissing.

And then of course you take up the flanks and guard the weakest point with people who have worked for years with publishers to select the few writers to speak for us—they're publisher-groupies who have conspired to work hard and manage who gets in and not. The browner your life in the Chicano world, the less chance you have of ever being published by a major publishing house. The less compliant you are, the more outspoken, the more you rage against the petty white publishers' game of choosing who is heard and who is silenced, the more censured, silenced, buried you'll be. *Asina es la cosa.*

Call me *cabezudo*, but I still don't think you can tell a writer what to write. Let her write what she wants. It's the publishers, here, that are pulling the strings, deciding who gets published or not, what gets paid or not. And Mexicans are free game. You can take anything you want from them, even their stories, their suffering, their dreams and pains. They don't have the capacity to think or write on their own. The immigrants are free game, as shown by border politics, placed in cages and fed like dogs, slaughtered by drug cartels, paid nothing for sweat labor in the fields. You can take everything from them, even their stories. And they come without baggage—they can't do anything to you.

Well, I read that the bookstores are packed. Her book is good for business. So the deluge of famous writers backing this book seems to be working. It fits perfectly on the shelf as a commodity that makes the mainstream book buyer feel so good about us Mexicans. We are somehow so corrupted and unable to tell our own story that it calls for a cultural heist by the publishers. Theirs is the truest version of our experience. Hollywood is grabbing as fast as the book gets published—it's easy to see why people prefer Taco Bell over the Mexican food truck parked at parks and work sites. You don't want to get contaminated with real Mexican food. Keep it corporate.

It is time for us to stand up and tell them to please keep their for-sale sign off our front lawns, to keep their fit-in specials out of our store windows. We don't need them anymore. Their nursery-rhyme promotions for a book no longer are essential to our sense of what we think a good book is. We measure our love of books by what our heart dictates: Does it move us? Does it change the way we see things? Does it shed new light on our journey? Does it give us some essential hope in these times? Does it bring deep appreciation for our humanity and our fragility and courage? Nothing empowers us like books that mock us.

Okay, well, so much for my paper. . . . So, Profe, I wrote this letter to beg you, to please, *por favor, Mano*, give me a good grade—a passing one. You can see that I thought a lot about the assignment. I just didn't know how to write about it. In love, *vato, tú sabes.*

And one more thing: my *reina* left me, went with another dude. So, can you please find it in your *corazón* to give me a good grade. A broken heart must merit at least that, *¿qué no?*

BLACK HEART

(with apologies to Ezra Pound)

A few months after I enrolled in school in Santa Luz, I met this woman in my class and we started dating. A remarkable woman. I've never known anyone like her and the more we dated and got serious about a relationship the more she opened up to me about her life.

Clara spent a year saving every penny from her waitress job at a high-end restaurant. After writing to Anaam for six months, she finally had the courage to move from Boston to Santa Luz, New Mexico. She'd never forget the day she climbed up the stairs to his apartment, knocked and stood for a while listening to someone behind the door cough, a harsh, lung-gasping cough as if the person was dying. Then the door opened, and there stood the hero of her life in his boxer shorts and T-shirt, unshaven, glaring at her, a cigarette burning in the ashtray on the windowsill that faced the street below. He hacked again, coughing up phlegm and grabbed the bottom hem of his T-shirt and spat the phlegm into it.

Anaam stuck his head out the door and peered down the hall-way both ways and said to her, "Didn't bring your lawyers and public relations manager, I see. Surprise, seems every fucking writer now has a lawyer and public relations team to defend their sexual harassment accusations . . . they don't shit unless they get permission from their lawyers."

Clara didn't understand what he was talking about. She looked around—every piece of furniture was made of stacks of books. His bed, table, side table with lamps, seats, were all made of books piled into neat towers and platforms. It was not what she expected of the greatest living poet, nor of a Mexican, since his name, Mr. Anaam Akaam, sure as hell wasn't Mexican, unless he was Mexican via Middle Eastern, Mediterranean or Arabic descent.

Anaam was muscular, strong in the way one might expect of a lumberjack. Clara would learn his daily habit of standing at the window and doing bench presses with hand barbells, 30 reps each arm, reclining on his weight bench made of books, and doing 30 reps of chest lifts. When he didn't go to the local Y to swim, he enjoyed running laps at the nearby park, where the Central Americans played soccer. He said he'd been running for forty years to help him think. He napped, a lot, had no set schedule for sleeping and waking. He slept whenever he wanted, ate whatever pleased him. His mood swings went from instantaneous combustion of elation to riveting interest in a poem to speechless silence when he didn't want to be bothered by anyone. Once a month he would get drunk. When neighborhood gangsters or derelicts or pseudo-intellectuals dropped by with drugs, cocaine, meth, weed, he'd roam his apartment naked with a woman thirty years younger and fuck her a thousand different ways. Then he'd sit on his bed of books and talk in flurries of things he was going to do, of a house he was going to buy, of living in the redwoods, of getting in touch with his five ex-wives and maybe having dinner with them. Everywhere you looked there were mountains of notebooks and loose-leaf journals and single sheets of half-finished poems and notes and numbers and ideas. He was always cursing.

When Clara asked him why he didn't apply for awards and grants like all the other poets and writers not as good as him did, he'd say that he refused to humiliate himself by taking rich people's money.

"Look around, don't you see what these silicon internet brats have done to this once beautiful city? After retiring, the Wall Street and law-firm guys that defend those crooks settle here and make this their geriatric ward. They've destroyed it with their sissiness and Bikram-Yoga crap and slender-fingered sensitivity workshops, where they have to be trained where to touch a woman because they can't fuck, they're so lame."

Some time back he had decided not to publish anymore, not in the magazines or with New York publishers; he considered them nothing more than corporate machines run by witless white and black liberals intent on wallowing in pop-culture trends or beckoning to the call of politically correct sirens who presumed to know the heart of a man or whose writers and poets were as tame as eunuchs.

"Go to the bookstore and you'll see all their books on the shelves, all dripping with sugary and pretentious gobbledygook. . . . No." Then, wagging his index finger at her, he'd say, "They're the death of poetry," and he'd add, "I am not one to sit on my haunches and *arf-arf* for nibbles from the master's hand."

"But," she would argue, "Mr. Anaam Akaam . . ." using his formal name to separate their friendship from the impending disagreement on a strictly literary point.

"This is not a discussion," he would break in. "I know every thing, you know nothing. You're all fluff and cotton candy, like the rest of them panting in line. Clara, every time an award is announced in one of the trade magazines for writers and poets, you turn the page hoping you'll win some money or prestige or approval. You're complicit in the madness of this incestuous literary orgy. It's like a late-night snack, and you're hungry and you flip the kitchen light on and open a cupboard, and cockroaches skitter everywhere. Turn the page, and cockroaches scamper every which way—that's how writers and poets scurry for the crumbs in the palms of philanthropists. They're cockroaches in the cupboard. . . . But that's okay, it is what it is."

Walking around the park with him or maybe sitting at one of the outside taco stands on the street, Clara would say, as his eyes followed a nice ass moving down the sidewalk, mesmerizing him, "You are too damn proud, you asshole. Or you're a cynical motherfucker."

"Cynical? Me?" he would say, food crumbs on his lips and shirt and week-old facial growth. "Blacks can't write shit unless it's acceptable to whites, and whites can't write unless it's acceptable to blacks. It's a sorry business. Nobody's writing real shit. The whole generation of iPhone and laptop poets, all with little experience at living, are after awards, recognition, to be applauded and hailed as great. That's not writing or poetry. And browns and Asians and shit . . . once they get a little something from the literary establishment, *YOUR HEROES,* and friends, I might add, turn into sexual predators. They can't pick up a woman on fair ground and equal terms, so they revert to sexual cannibalism, eating their own kind: Native American women and Caribbean women. . . . That fucking Indian, what's his name, and that wimpy fucking Dominican? . . . It takes a real bitch to force oneself on a younger female writer looking for a mentor, all the while these friends of yours self-consciously posture themselves as bad-ass men. Well, yes, I guess they are your kind of men. Get real, Clara. Now pay for our tacos."

"Sure, since you spit half of yours at me while talking."

He farted in the grocery line, on the street, in close quarters, it didn't matter. He cursed in public, cried out to dot-commers in suits on the street, calling them faggots and capitalists and pigs and murderers. And when she tried to tell him to please stop, he'd reply, "Who's going to arrest a seventy-five-year-old man? Get real, Clara."

"I am real. I've been your friend for some time now and I've seen you fuck off your gift on drugs and whiskey and cheap flings. I've seen you and loved you and worried over you and wondered the whole time, Don't you know you have a gift, but don't respect it and . . ."

"Oh, yes, I hire you to be my intern, and what do you do? Become my nursemaid, my guru? Huh? You bring this shit on post-ums, telling so-and-so to talk to me. . . ."

"I volunteer to be your intern. You don't pay me."

"That's irrelevant. I hire you, and you bring this crap. Listen to what I tell you, and you might become a poet one day."

ৼ৹ ৫৶

"You wanna hear the truth? Ha!" he said after they entered the Y and he got into his weightlifting. "When 9/11 happens, I tell them fuck themselves. On CNN, MSNBC, PBS, CBS and FOX, on radio programs, including shows on NPR, CBC and Sirius XM, print and online newspapers and magazines including *Time*, *USA Today* and the *Los Angeles Times*, *The New York Times* and *Huffington Post*, the *Washington Post* and *The Atlantic*.

"They ask me to be on, and I tell them, they don't want me because I will say it's our fault, after all the shit we have done to them, stealing their resources, propping up dictators and raping their women and shit. Of course, they hang up. And we call ourselves men . . . sending tanks and rockets and drones against children with stones—big, big men we are. Those Israelis committing all kinds of atrocities against people they contain in a concentration camp while they steal their land—real honorable people, and all with American blessings.

"Capitalism is an inhuman machine with its own menu. It will not eat the heart of a bull. No, it must have it with antibiotics and spices, corrupted and infected with our bacteria, made foul by our cowardice. . . . We lost our bull's honor and courage in this manner. You have to eat it while it still beats, bite while the blood still pulses through its ventricles. . . . But can you imagine a fat-assed white Christian midwestern housewife doing that?"

"Enough, Anaam, fuck you. I'm leaving. You always go off when I try to talk seriously to you about your career. Stew in your own bitter madness."

"I'll see you later on tonight, love you."

ᥫᥬ ᥬᥫ

She would never be as gifted as Anaam. Everything he wrote was great. He had a cult following, matched in number by his haters. At poetry readings, women in the front rows often lifted their shirts to reveal a tattoo of one of his poems on their breasts, bellies or arms. One man even had a poem tattooed on his face, the last line, "GAME OVER," tattooed to his eyelids.

Once, the organizers for the Denver Book Festival invited him to read but purposely omitted his name from the schedule. When he was supposed to read and walked into the auditorium, there were five hundred empty seats. Unfazed, Anaam told Clara to take a seat and read aloud for an hour. There sat Clara in the middle of vast sea of empty chairs, and this old man on stage reading, flailing his arms, pausing his voice for effect, looking over the hundreds of faces that weren't there, roaring as if they were all listening to him.

Maybe it was the movies he wrote that fucked him up, maybe book after book that came out hailed with quiet awe, maybe his disregard for convention, his spurious cannon-exploding ill temper toward anything slightly or remotely resembling compliance. He said writers these days were a sad lot. Were he leading a workshop, he claimed, he would send them all to the hills to starve for a month, he would have them sit naked before courthouses to protest the inhumane treatment of children, he would have them tutor illiterate children, teach them grammar and such, he would . . . And they turned on him, small-spirted slaves to the almighty patrons of the arts and their checkbooks.

Anaam told a story about Bukowski and Sean Penn, how Penn one day asked Bukowski to be his mentor. Bukowski had been drinking that morning (surprise), was still in his boxer shorts and wife-beater and asked Sean to wait at the door while he went to put on his combat boots. Then, facing Penn, he said, "Bend down and kiss these boots." When Penn did, Bukowski scowled that no poet would ever do that and slammed the door in his face. And thus, we have Penn the actor.

Anaam's stories, at their core, vibrated with universal meaning and often made Clara wonder whether she was just another loud-mouthed wannabe like 90% of writers and poets in America. What if, as Anaam posed the question to her one day, when a poet was required to read his poem aloud to the public and it was rejected, the public stoned and executed him? "How many poets would be writing?" he asked.

"That's the kind of criteria we need, Clara. Not this Iowa Writers' Workshop crap, where once you attend, you have instant approval and awards and money. Same with Naropa. All beads and meditation and being cool. Stone them, burn them, bad writers, bad literature, bad poetry . . . there is no greater crime, my friend."

She could never understand his sadness, his begrudging existence, his not wanting to live, his not wanting to be subjected to establishment politics and societal norms. Sometimes when she arrived at his apartment, she'd hear loud mystical music playing and find him sitting on the floor naked, chanting a mantra, his grubby face sublime and enchanted. Lost in another world, he would sit and sing as if angels had possessed him, as if he were somewhere close to God, at the foot of God, praying in his scratchy voice.

Maybe Allen Ginsberg was right when he wrote in his famous poem, *Howl*: "I saw the best minds of my generation destroyed by madness, starving hysterical naked."

సౌ ౷

Often, after a day of straightening out his papers and collat-
ing his poems chronologically, she would leave his apartment and
walk down the street, worried that he could hardly breathe anymore. Yet, he'd stand at the open window yelling at her for all the
world to hear that poets do not have fucking careers. "Don't ever
say the word 'poet' around me again or I'll career your ass, shove
it up as far as it'll go, and you'll be shitting career for the next two
months. . . ."

cᐁ ᐁↄ

Before leaving Boston, so happy that he had accepted her re-
quest to study under him, she had to agree to sign what he called
his manifesto, his Bill of Rights. She sat at her table and read his
"Poet's Proclamation":

I will never be a ladder-climbing people-pleaser.

*I will never be a bookmark-flattering rehab-elite with mim-
icries of others' messages.*

*I will never be a skirt-hemming pincher, knee-dipping curt-
sier to the queen-bee for a moneyed nest.*

*I will never be a sweet-talking networking courier or scut-
tling errand-maid for the rich.*

*I will never be a back-biting company charmer, campaigning
for a literary post.*

*I will never be an award-mongering grubber nor paper-poet
applicant or cup-rattler for institutional favor.*

*I will never be an expatriate slouching in a Mexican resort or
TV personality Tame-Tongue sipping lattés at a Sunset Boule-
vard café, pleading with a host for airtime on NPR or PBS.*

*I will never cash in my dreams and become a literary cheek-
rubber and hee-hawing yawper just for a chance to teach at a
university or wear the leafy crown of poet laureate.*

She was dumbfounded. At the bottom of his letter, he added a postscript:

From what you have told me about yourself, you are a bastard born and bred from prairie pinto beans and chile verde. *By swearing an oath of loyalty to your grandparent's memory, you vow to adhere to your mission. At this moment, were you to enter the lofty halls of academia, so large is your renewed resolve, you'd be certain to bump the top of door frames, and so great your intellect, you'd have to stoop to enter the shabby recovery rooms of meager minds.*

Despite reading these ramblings, she felt herself in the presence of a great poet.

༺ ༻

After a year with Anaam, she was accepted into a writing program in Maine, and she left Santa Luz and Anaam for six months. When she returned, he was gone. The apartment had been abandoned in a hurry—Spam and Potted Meat cans half used still cluttered his bookshelves and counters. She asked the neighbors about him, and they said he had been arrested. When she checked with the police at the area station, they told her he had been transferred to an asylum in Las Vegas, New Mexico. She asked what his crime was, and they informed her he was a danger to himself. Because they could not find any relatives, the state had taken custody and institutionalized him.

Clara went to the asylum to visit him, but they wouldn't allow her in. She waited for days, sleeping in her car outside the fenced-in exercise area until one day she spotted him shuffling about in sandals and wearing a patient's smock. He was mumbling to himself, gesturing at the air, referring to a book in his hands that wasn't there, turning pages and reciting poems from it. He would raise his head in grand nodding acknowledgement that he was right on the question he posed to himself.

Clara went up to the fence and called to him, waving her arms and motioning him to come over.

"Amaan, Amaan, what happened? I've missed you, my friend, so much. I'll get you out, I promise, whatever it takes, you won't stay here."

He smiled, pointed his finger at her, waved and then returned to his invisible book and walked away.

Clara cried. Her fingers clutched the cyclone fence so she wouldn't fall. As she sat in her car staring at him in the enclosed area, she remembered their days together. Her memories overcame her like a leviathan wave, yielding so much light it obscured the sky. As she stared, Anaam looked like a blue whale rising with enough force to launch itself out of the water and turn in the air, casting its shadow over a seashell on the beach—she was that seashell.

Clara could not explain why, but for all his eccentricities, he was the sole, sane element in her otherwise miserable life. He grounded her with his truth, affirmed her belief that beyond the cities and fields and oceans, he was there with his clarity and space and truth and reality. He had straightened her out.

Clara had been offered a tenured position to teach poetry at the Naropa Institute, and she intended to take it until that day she went to visit him. She'd been leaning toward sacrificing her dream of being a real poet, one who did not give up her standards, who did not feel compelled to compromise her principles as a once fiery and unyielding dreamer-poet into becoming an obsolete cardboard-box effigy dangling from the department head's puppet strings.

Seeing Anaam in that cage walking back and forth, talking to invisible legions of poets, she realized how out of sheer boredom and frustration she was willing to go along with the gaggle of hacks and how they went about their business of getting published and making an ass-kissing career for themselves. But seeing him that day changed that. She didn't want to be a derivative or to take up someone else's slack, mimic them, live off their legacy, curtsy her way to the top.

Despite being weary of poverty, of her dependence on graduate grants and loans and isolation, she had decided she was back to her insane but beautiful original self, with her original passion to live the mystic's life, abscond into the esthetic wilderness and lose herself in her poetic reveries, as Anaam was now doing in his own way.

Back at his apartment, Clara decided to stay and go through all his boxes and organize his work into some kind of sane inventory with the hopes of giving it to a university library for archival study. While doing so, one day she came upon a box filled with letters to her that he had forgotten to mail or simply decided not to.

She skipped around from one to another, as certain paragraphs caught her interest:

June 25th, 2017

The recent trend toward poor-me books is flooding the market, with academic poets and writers affecting a feminine posture on the one hand, and when on stage, morphing into a mix of John Wayne and Rambo, cursing and cussing and throwing themselves out to the public as the new outlaw poets.

Sept. 7th, 2017

I think if you listen intently to your heart, it'll give you something. It's a crazy thing. . . . I gave my book, even after I sent you the version I did, I gave it one more slap, and bingo, I hit the chords I wanted on half a dozen very specific passages that were bothering me. But listen, if nothing bothers you about this, go with it, just that when I did my last spotty revision, I felt an overwhelming sense that I had answered the call of my heart and what it was trying to tell me. I felt it.

Just the way I see the sunrise coming over the city here where I sit, I lay on my side and watch the sun hit a distant sky-rise on the west side. Slowly it comes into sight—not the rising sun to the east, but what it hits when it creeps over the eastern side and burns far away on the west. And I lay here and watch it slowly illuminate this incredibly lovely land. Then it's time to get up and it helps me climb out of bed and meet the day with all its crazy trails that often make us stop to catch our breath and feel our fraternity with all living energy.

Here's what it is—when you start your book, Clara, the first page is the rising sun, barely peeking over, telling you that you have some business to take care of, and after some minutes the city becomes visible in its misty, shrouded way, and then the west suddenly is on fire and tells you get on with it, it lights you up like a fire sparking in your gristle and knees and shoulders and neck and stomach and fingers, spreading across all the pages of the book, one beautiful smooth spreading of light that finds its culmination on the last page.

Just think about it, be patient, let it ride in your bones for a few days, keep thinking on it as you move through the day.

Sept. 11th, 2017

I chose you, Clara, because you've painted yourself into a corner, forced yourself to be honest with yourself. As you stand in that corner, tigers roam the room waiting for you to make a move. Or there's a fire in the room, and you stand in the corner crouching as the flames come toward you. Or the room is being squeezed in a press, or a vice, and everything's getting closed in and there's a sense that you better do something, or you'll be crushed to death. That's where the poem comes in, the only thing that can calm the tigers is the poem, the only thing to douse the flames is the poem, the only thing to stop the walls and ceiling from crushing you alive is the poem and its magic and its release of a transcendent power that raises you above mediocrity. The poem matters, it marrows the gut and splits the tendons like banjo strings, arises, and with it, so does your freedom.

I don't want "poets" in my life. I want people who need to tell a story, for whatever reason. It's a life thing: something in them drives them with incessant whispers and hisses and snarls and claws to tell what they sense in the dark of their lives. Fuck "writers" and fuck "poets"— most of them anyway. There's more telling in the frayed and torn and patched overcoat of a Mexican weed runner than in most so-called poets. . . . What we're suffering from in this country are nickel-bag poets who are led by the nose-ring of a huff and puff career. They slow-bleed out their poetry with comfortable arrangements, cordial obedience, until whatever ambivalence exists in their brains drains into sour-canned yessums on the academic shelf next to the potted meat.

Sept. 11th, 2017

Take away from your visit a re-commitment to re-ignite the "I can" spark in yourself. If it's dim, blow on your dream to lead others into the light, rekindle your dream from a time when life blazed with possibilities, blow on the fire of purpose or meaning of learning's light and share its beauty, step into your dream again and feed the fire again so the flame of your own potential personhood in this world shines with brilliant illumination again. You are the coveted fire you offer us, so we might in turn carry it and pass it on.

But it starts with you.

Carry away from your visit the unwavering belief and certainty that you are hero and messenger, you are the seed-planting people, going heart to heart and mind to mind, planting the divine kernels in each person of what they have forgotten: who they can be in this world. From where you sit, if you were to take your finger and trace all the way back to where you came from as a child, and remember your dream to be a poet, remember why you wanted to be a poet, then you will see yourself again filled with awe at life, filled with supreme faith that the world is good and filled with the beautiful light of learning.

Poetry best manifests itself in a poet's ability to build a healthy, community-serving life. Poetry should be the footstool that allows each to affirm his or her best traits. A good poet creates an environment to transform what is unjust, to heal those searching and lost. Poetry allows the poet to wage his talents and compassionate heart against destructive forces in our society. A poet creates words to demolish the obstacles all of us face in making a more generous society. And it is you, right now this very moment, who carries the keys to make this marvelous revolution possible, to shape this transcendent crop of young minds and hearts rising from the field like a heady sunflower reaching for the sun. It is you who teach to bend but never break, you who foster faith in themselves, you who teach them to stay strong and determined, and they will arrive because you are a living and breathing testimony and witness as my fellow poet, because you sit before me here today.

You have so many stories to share. And in that pursuit, my amazing young poet, your life has been a narrative of service to others, not for fame or fortune, but as a leader on a journey to fulfill your creative potential, to help you realize your vision in its healthiest and mindful way of serving your community of humanity.

Ultimately, you are the keeper of the keys, of secrets you share with others who are wide-eyed and innocent, some shy and fearful, others unable to sit for more than a few minutes, always bouncing around and inattentive, but still, you help others shape themselves into courageous human beings and leaders.

Thank you for teaching me, thank you for walking beside me, for riding the rough days with me, for captaining the ship of my life in stormy hurricanes, for respecting this precious cargo called my heart, the heaven-made box transporting my dreams and me, day by day, for you are the one who gave me direction, you are the one who taught me to read the stars in my heart and write down what they meant, what I was capable of, who I was, where I was going and what I could achieve, you star-reader, mapmaker, compass needle, that kept me safely on the trail on my way to my life.

Nov. 16th, 2017

Let's make our poetry the space where we can say the hardest truths and make the most painful revelations about ourselves. It's time to turn our poetry into the battleground for our souls and minds and futures. It is where we become, we grow, we shape our identities, we learn to love and hate and get angry. Poems will be the nests from which we gain the courage to fly . . . but right now we are taught to fear, to never test our wings, to never take a risk. . . .

I think poets define where the line is—and if we don't, we should. We are leaders, and our poems will one day encompass the world. What we say will be listened to. Leagues of people will align with us, and we will define the future. We have power we haven't tested or even entrusted to ourselves. Poets are the leaders, and we have to understand that we can make change for the better, we can force the hand of politicians, we can demand our voices be heard. . . .

We are here because this is where there is so much political unrest. We blossom where there is drought, we embrace liberty where there are walls, we clutch hands where there are clenched fists . . . this is who we are. Where there is strife and racism and poverty and domestic violence and addiction, we are there—that is who we are. We come bearing knowledge, we carry within us a special awareness that informs us of ourselves in the world, that informs us of our value and purpose. We go into the world pulling our brothers and sisters from the bottom of history to make them no longer dishwashers or laborers but makers of history. We drag them forth using language to succor their wounds. We lure them out to trust us and to teach them to use language as a weapon to fight lies, to destroy deception, to open the world with truth—that is who we are.

You sit there in your graduate classes, but I know who you are. . . . You are a dream maker—not dragon slayer, but bigger, more important, more essential to our communities. What you slay has no eyes or hands or face, yet it sits before you every day trying to take innocent youth away. You know what to fight it with, what weapons, how to fight it, how to keep that young poet from going with it. Your weapons have always been reading. The first time you read, a poem made your world less fearful and less dangerous and made you more powerful and brave. That is what you offer to protect the youth, that's your magic. Reading. Against this enemy that has no body and works tirelessly to kidnap youth, you plunge your hands into history and drag up the young poet and bring that poet to the forefront to create history, not be a victim of it. And when it returns using nefarious tactics, you strike your sword of language, weaponize your words to fight injustice, to fight racism, by using words that burn with your consciousness and commitment to healthier communities. You give your young poets the weapons, the tools, the confidence, the love, the hope to rise up from despair, to slough off and shake away the chains of illiteracy—that's what you do.

Clara almost never left Anaam's apartment, reading all day and night, and when she did, it was to eat at the same joints they used to frequent; the Asian noodle place with the yellow neon light, the Cuban and Argentinian place with cracks in the wall, or down alleys, drinking cheap beer and eating tacos sitting on a green-painted bench. Months later when she finally finished going through all his papers and manuscripts, she convinced Stanford to acquire his archives. With the money they gave her, she was able to hire a private nurse for Anaam and fill his room with books. Stanford placed his papers between the archives of Hemingway and Levertov in the Special Collections library.

Clara decided to sublease Anaam's apartment. Now, she teaches poetry at an alternative local high school, and at night, if you pass on the street and look up, you'll find her in her apartment, lifting barbells at the window or sitting at a table constructed of books, writing poems or reading.

There's a poem she found of Anaam's in a box that she liked so much she taped it to the wall in the main room where it can be seen from any place she's standing.

BLACK HEART

You criticize I am always in a foul mood
Here is my answer:

My heart is black and charred.
You assume I don't know
how to handle fire,
it's out of control
(you say, meaning my emotions).

I reply no, it's just my desires
are too much for my heart to contain.
They burn fierce, they flare,
the flames reach to the stars.

Hence, my heart is charred
all around the outside,
an *horno* fireplace opening stuffed
with too much kindling
where desires broke free
from my heart's boundaries,
and flames reached beyond
their accustomed space
out to the unknown for their dream.

A black heart is evidence of a dreamer,
my friend, burning with too much light.